The Reckoning

Lone Rider Novel, 1

Rusty Beauquet

SIX-GUN WESTERN HERITAGE PRESS

ISBN 979-8-2012774-0-6

Contents

"I ride alone, but never alone.

I carry the fallen in my heart always.

Many miles have they traveled with me."

— by Ty Alvarez, a poem

In memory of my great-grandfather, H. R. Darter, a true western man.

Chapter 1

The Lone Rider

A LONE RIDER ON a long-legged roan came to Dead Horse Crossing on the Pecos. He was a gray-eyed man wearing a black high-crowned, wide-brimmed hat, blue cotton shirt under a brown leather vest, and brown wool pants. He was riding easy when the people of the town first noticed him, but his horse was dust-coated with dried sweat showing on the flanks and top of the rump. The stranger rode directly to the stable, dismounted, and paid the liveryman to care for his horse.

Only after seeing to the care of his horse did he turn and glance toward the hotel. Then he crossed the hard-packed dirt street, pulling his hat brim down lower and adjusting the tied-down Colt at his right hip. Two cowboys sitting in chairs in the shade out front stood as the stranger approached. They crossed the rough-hewn plank porch, spurs jingling, and met him at the front door. One of them, a heavyset fellow, tipped his sweat-stained hat back on his head.

"Something I can do for you, stranger?"

"You run this hotel?" the new arrival asked.

"No."

"Then there's nothing you can do for me," the man said before opening the door and entering the lodging establishment.

Inside, he strode to the front desk and tapped the bell on the counter. A clerk sauntered out of a backroom, looking the stranger up and down.

"Yes?"

"I'd like a room."

"Sorry, mister, we're all full up."

The stranger spun the guest register around on the counter and flipped through some pages.

"You seem to have lots of vacancies."

"Well, uh, some cattlemen are due to arrive any time now, and they spoke for most of the vacant rooms. And we reserve the few rooms left for the pleasure and comfort of the local cowboys when they come into town from the ranches. They pay for the rooms in advance by the week or month."

The stranger glanced at a board nailed to the wall to the side of the desk, where room keys hung in rows from brass hooks. He selected a key and showed the numbered tag to the clerk.

"I'll take this one," the man said. He picked up a pencil from the counter and signed his name on the register. "I'd like to have a bath if it's not too much trouble."

The desk clerk turned and pointed to the stairs. "Head of the stairs. I'll bring some water up."

When the front door opened, the stranger looked over his shoulder. The lanky, raw-boned cowboy sitting outside with the heavyset man when he had arrived walked in. The man strolled over to a chair, sat down, and crossed his legs. He pulled out the makings, rolled a cigarette, and produced a match. He struck it against the bottom of his boot and lit the smoke, his eyes never leaving the stranger.

Key in hand, the stranger walked toward the stairs but paused in front of the cowboy.

"Don't know why you're so interested, but the name is McNeil. It's all in the register," he said. Then he turned away and mounted the stairs to the second floor.

The cowboy stood and crossed the room to the counter.

"Pete McNeil, Uvalde, Cotton," the clerk said without prompting.

The cowboy nodded and leaned on the counter. "I want to know everything he does, where he goes, and who he talks to, Jay."

"Okay, Cotton. But what do we do in the meantime?"

"In the meantime, I think I'll see how easy McNeil is to push."

When McNeil left his room with a towel for the bath, he met the desk clerk in the hallway carrying two buckets of hot water. He waited until the man dumped the water into the copper tub. Then, when the clerk departed, he went inside, closed the door, and undressed. McNeil climbed into the tub and scrubbed off the trail dust using a bar of lye soap.

McNeil padded barefoot back down the hallway to his room, wearing the towel around his waist and with his clothes and boots bundled under his arm. His gun belt hung over his shoulder. He opened the door, went in, and found the cowboy from downstairs reclined on the bed, smoking.

"I guess maybe you're in the wrong room," McNeil said.

"You think so? What else you got on your mind?"

"Well, nothing else, I guess," McNeil said, dropping his bundled clothes on the washstand and his boots on the floor.

"If you had any sense, you would have listened to what Jay downstairs told you. He said most of the vacant rooms here are all spoken for by the cattlemen on the way to town. The rest of the rooms, the hotel reserves for the pleasure and comfort of us cowboys."

"So, I guess this is your room?"

"It is when I'm in town, and as any fool can see, I'm in town right now. You can see that, can't you, McNeil?"

"I guess so."

"Where you from, McNeil?"

McNeil jerked his thumb towards the southeast.

"Where you headed?"

McNeil pointed toward the northwest.

"I guess you're a man of few words, McNeil."

"That makes one of us. I try to live a quiet, contemplative life. Talking too much interferes with that. So, you know my name. What's yours?"

"Cotton Patrick. I ride for the Bar Deuce spread outside of town. I answered your question, so answer one for me. What are you doing in Dead Horse Crossing?"

"I'm not huntin' trouble, but that's my business. It's a free country, the last I heard. We even fought a big war not long ago to emphasize the point. So I figure I have as much right to rent a room in this fine hotel as the next man."

"But not my room, you don't. A room I've already rented. And I believe a man's nothing unless he stands up for what's rightfully his, McNeil. What do you think?"

"I guess so."

"You're all the time guessing, McNeil. Don't you know anything?"

"Well, I know everyone has been downright inhospitable ever since I rode into this town. Mind telling me why?"

"I guess I rightfully don't know. But the way I see it, it looks a mite suspicious when a man rides into town and refuses to answer a few simple questions. Makes people think he has something to hide."

Ignoring the remark, McNeil said, "Well, if this is your room, Patrick, I guess you won't mind me gathering my things so I can go get another one."

The cowboy looked at the gun belt slung over McNeil's shoulder, positioned so that the butt of the Colt was close to hand.

"You a gun hand, are you, McNeil?"

"You know as well as I do, Patrick, most men in this country wear guns same as they wear pants. That doesn't make them all gunmen. But if it makes you feel any better, I'm a cowpuncher by trade, just like you."

"So, you here looking for work, McNeil? Maybe I could introduce you to the foreman at the Bar Deuce."

"I'm not huntin' a job or lookin' for any trouble, Patrick. I'm just passing through."

Patrick swung his legs off the bed and stood. "I guess you can have the room, McNeil, seeing how you already got the key. And I expect you won't be in town long since you're just passing through."

"Yeah, I'll probably be on my way by tomorrow afternoon. Now, if you don't mind, I'd like to get dressed and go find some grub for supper."

"Sure, don't let me hold you up. See you around, McNeil. Patrick sauntered over to the door, went out, and closed the door behind him."

McNeil wondered why everyone in the two-bit town of Dead Horse Crossing seemed on the prod. He had nothing to hide. But maybe someone in the town did. Something they wanted to keep secret. Maybe by whatever means it took.

Chapter 2

An Unfriendly Town

McNEIL, BATHED AND DRESSED in clean clothes, descended the stairs to the hotel lobby. He saw that Cotton Patrick was back sitting in the same chair as before, smoking. Sitting in another chair beside Patrick was the heavyset cowboy McNeil had spoken to briefly and brushed past on his way into the hotel. There was a third loafer in the lobby now, an older man wearing a worn derby atop his graying head, a white broadcloth shirt with a western tie, and dark wool pants. The man glanced furtively at McNeil and then turned away to resume staring out the window. The hotel clerk was behind the front desk, leaning on it. It felt to McNeil that his appearance had interrupted a conversation among the men assembled in the lobby. As McNeil crossed the plank floor to the door, the hotel man called out.

"Hey, hold it a minute, Mr. McNeil."

McNeil stopped and turned. "Yeah?"

"How long you staying?" the clerk said.

"In my room, you mean?"

"I mean this hotel."

"Why are you asking? You expecting a run on rooms?"

"I was just asking. I'll need time to get that room ready again before the cattlemen arrive."

McNeil looked at the clerk and sighed tiredly. "Twenty-four hours, maybe." Then he turned and strolled out the front door.

Three riders rode up fast to the front of the hotel, reined in their mounts, and dismounted in the dust cloud they had stirred up. The men tied their horses to the hitching rail. Two looked like ranch hands, but the third, a large, thick-necked man, wore fancier duds. McNeil stepped off the plank walk onto the street to find his passage blocked suddenly by the three men. It seemed they had stepped in front of him intentionally for that purpose.

"Here we go again," McNeil said to no one in particular. Then, with the ghost of a smile on his lips, he skirted the three men and continued walking down the dusty street. All three turned and watched him go for a moment before mounting the steps to the wood sidewalk and hurrying toward the hotel's front door.

In the lobby, Patrick and the three others were all standing at the window watching the departing McNeil when the three riders walked into the hotel. The big, well-dressed man strode right to the counter. He spun the guest register around and peered down at it. The desk clerk sidled over to the desk and stopped beside him.

"That's all I know about him, Mr. Sommers. He rode in this afternoon and made me rent him a room even after I told him we were full up."

Ignoring the clerk, the man turned and looked at the backs of Patrick and the other cowboy as they continued staring out the front window. The big man's eyes hardened almost imperceptibly as the older man approached him.

"Sit down, Grover."

The hefty cowboy turned and said, "I was only—"

"I said sit down. You too, Cotton."

The men moved from the window and reclaimed the chairs where they had sat earlier before McNeil's exit. The two cowboys who had arrived with Sommers leaned against the wall near the front door with their arms crossed, snickering.

"How are you, Doc?" the big man said, acknowledging the older man.

"Can't complain, Bull. How are you?"

"Passably well, thanks."

Then Bull Sommers turned his attention to Cotton Patrick. Patrick spoke up without prompting.

"He's one cool customer."

"He doesn't push easily?" Sommers said.

"That's the thing. He pushes too easy. I took a run at him upstairs in his room. He was all polite like and wouldn't rise to the bait I was using. But I saw it in his eyes."

"Saw what?"

"No fear, not a mite. He doesn't strike me as a man who runs from a fight, and I expect he's handy with the tied-down Colt he wears. Despite his words, he stood there looking amused the whole time. He put me in mind of a coiled rattlesnake ready to strike. Maybe we ought to—"

Sommers waved a hand impatiently and turned back to the older man.

"What do you think, Doc?"

"Nothing. I'm just wondering why you are all so lathered up about one stranger? He seems to me like a common drifter just passing through."

Sommers eyed the man coldly. "You wonder too much, and you ask too many questions. That's not a winning hand, Doc."

"It's just that there seems no cause for concern about that stranger unless you only look at him from a certain point of view."

"How do you look at him?"

"With the innocence of a freshly born calf," Doc said.

"Keep it up, Doc," Sommers said. "Maybe you'll say something funny one day. Or, maybe I'll have Grover Rhodes wash your mouth out with soap."

Chastened, Doc made no reply. Sommers brushed past him, crossed the room to the window, and looked out.

"He's going into the jail," Sommers said with irritation.

McNeil opened the door and stepped into the jail. Unlike the others in town, wooden buildings with false fronts, the jail was a squat, rock structure made of sandstone that McNeil figured the builders had quarried nearby. The interior was untidy and smelled of stale sweat and cheap whiskey. There was a shopworn desk in one corner of the dimly lighted room with an empty, worn wooden chair behind it. McNeil saw a wooden rack holding two Winchesters and a double-barrel scattergun on the wall behind the desk. Wanted posters of yellowed, curled paper tacked to the wall provided the only decorative touches. At the back was a heavy wood door that was standing open. From beyond it, McNeil heard snoring. He crossed the room and looked inside the backroom. There was a single cell with iron bars, its door standing open with a key in the lock. Asleep on the bunk inside the cell was a balding man of middle age and obvious mediocrity. Pinned on the chest of the man's dirty shirt was a silver star.

McNeil walked to the cell and slammed the door shut. The clang of steel on steel reverberated throughout the enclosed space. The sleeping man's eyes shot open. He sat up, jumped off the bunk, and sprang for the door. When he pushed on the bars, the door swung open on its squeaky hinges. Relieved, the man looked at McNeil with a sheepish grin.

"I wasn't hankering getting locked in my own jail cell."

McNeil registered the sickly smell of whiskey on the man's breath and his bloodshot eyes. It seemed the lawman had been sleeping off a drunk.

McNeil smiled. "Sorry, I thought you were a guest, and someone forgot to lock the door."

"No, I'm the host. I'm Bud Long, the town marshal."

"My name is McNeil."

"It's stuffy in here," Long said. "Let's go out to my office to palaver."

McNeil followed the marshal through the doorway into the office. Long sat down behind the desk, rubbing his watery eyes.

"You the fellow who rode into town this afternoon?" Without waiting for a reply, Long continued. "Old Sam, the liveryman, came over and told me about you after you boarded your horse and before he rode out to tell... Well, uh, never mind about that."

Long opened a desk drawer and took out a near-empty whisky bottle. He uncorked it and started to take a pull. But remembering his manners, stopped and offered the bottle to McNeil.

"Care for a snort?"

"No, thanks."

"Don't blame you. It tastes something awful," Long said before drinking from the bottle. He corked the bottle, smacking his lips, and set it on the desk.

"What are you lookin' at?" Long said in a stern tone.

"You tell me."

"I ain't always this bad. Last night, my friend Doc Holder and I played cards and drank too much. At least I did."

"You mean you played cards alone while he watched, or you were the only one who drank too much?"

"Don't get smart with me, McNeil. I'm the law in this town. What do you want?"

"I came in... "

"You ain't from around here, are you?" Long said. "You from down South Texas way? Are you one of the cattlemen we've been expecting?"

"No," McNeil said with a sigh. Then, as though speaking to a dull child, he continued. "All I want from you, Marshal, is a little information. I need to get out to a ranch located around here, the Lazy E. Can you direct me?"

Long reacted as though McNeil had slapped him. "This ain't the information bureau," he stammered.

"One thing about Dead Horse Crossing," McNeil said. "Everyone is so gracious and helpful. It must make for pleasant living."

"No one asked you to come here," Long retorted.

"How do you know no one asked me to come here, Marshal?" McNeil said with a rueful grin.

"What about the Lazy E?"

"I'm looking for the owner, Denton Everhart."

Long grabbed for the whiskey bottle. In his haste, he knocked it over, and it rolled toward the edge of the desk. Quick as a rattler's strike, McNeil reached out and caught the bottle an instant before it rolled off the desk to smash on the stone floor.

"That was a near disaster," he said, setting the bottle back upright on the desk.

"You're telling me," Long said, taking hold of the bottle with care and then uncorking it. He swallowed the rest of the whiskey.

Long eyed the tied-down Colt. "I barely saw your hand move when you grabbed the bottle. It was a blur. You move pretty fast. Are you a gun hand, McNeil?"

McNeil ignored the question and asked his own. "What about Everhart? You going to tell me how to find his spread?"

"If you have no further questions, I'm pretty busy," Long said.

With a shadow of a smile, McNeil said, "It seems clear I'll get no answers, Marshal. So, I guess I'll move along."

McNeil turned and went out the front door. Long watched him go. Then he reached for the whiskey bottle. He paused, noticing the bottle was empty, and withdrew his hand. Then he sat in the chair staring blindly ahead, seeing nothing except memories of some past terrible events.

Chapter 3

The Pressure Builds

Frowning and deep in thought, McNeil walked back up the dusty street toward the hotel. When he arrived, he climbed the steps to the wooden sidewalk. Looking down the way, he saw a sign advertising: Kate's Home Cooking. As McNeil passed the hotel headed for the eating establishment, Bull Sommers stepped out the hotel's front door, blocking his path.

"Afternoon, Mr. McNeil."

"That's the friendliest word I've had since I got here."

Sommers flashed a tight smile. "My name's Sommers. I own the Bar Deuce ranch outside of town."

Sommers extended his hand, and McNeil shook it.

"I want to apologize for some folks in town that haven't acted neighborly."

"People in this town act like they're sitting on something."

"Sitting on something? What exactly?"

"I don't know. A box of dynamite or a keg of gunpowder, maybe."

"Oh, no, nothing like that," Sommers said with a disarming smile. "They're just a little suspicious of strangers. That's all. I can tell you're a Texan. You know how it is with folks in small towns sometimes."

"I always thought the Texas tradition was hospitality."

"I'm trying to be hospitable, Mr. McNeil. You going to be in town a while?"

"Could be."

"How would you like to come out to the ranch tomorrow and see the place? I'd be proud to have you as my guest, and I'll have my cook prepare you a good meal."

"Thanks, all the same, but I guess not."

Sommers' face flushed. "Why not?" he demanded. "You have more important business to attend to in Dead Horse Crossing?"

"Could be. But I appreciate the kind invitation. I hope I haven't offended you."

Sommers' expression softened.

"No offense taken. If there's anything I can do for you while you're in town..."

"Well, there is one thing, maybe. I'm looking for a—never mind, but thanks anyway."

"You're looking for what, Mr. McNeil?" Sommers growled.

"A man named Everhart. He owns a ranch hereabouts, the Lazy E. I'm trying to find out how to get there from town. I suppose you're acquainted with the other ranchers around these parts."

"Everhart? Sure, I knew him."

"Knew him? You mean he isn't around anymore?"

"Everhart died."

"When?"

"Oh, maybe six months ago."

"Six months ago? You're sure about that?"

Sommers nodded. "I attended the funeral." Then, turning, Sommers pointed into the distance. "He's up there in the town cemetery. Cholera got him."

"Was there a break out here?"

"No, nothing like that. I heard Everhart went down to Mexico to buy some horses. Doc Holder says he probably picked it up down there. The Doc says cholera is a common malady south of the border."

McNeil studied Sommers keenly. Then he took a folded envelope from his pocket.

"This is a letter Everhart sent to his sister. The date at the top of the letter is from three months ago."

Sommers gave McNeil a hard look but said nothing.

"So, I guess there is nothing you can do for me, after all." McNeil brushed past the rancher and continued toward the sign advertising grub down the boardwalk.

Sommers stormed back into the hotel lobby. Patrick, Rhodes, Doc, the hotel man, and the two cowboys that rode in with Sommers gathered in a tight group around the rancher.

"What did he have to say?" Rhodes said.

Sommers glared at Rhodes, deciding whether the question challenged his authority. He concluded not and addressed the group.

"He asked about Everhart and the Lazy E."

"I don't like it," Patrick said.

"Maybe it's like he said, and he's just passing through," Rhodes said.

"Don't bet on it," Patrick retorted. "He can only mean trouble."

"Cotton, you're as jumpy as a stall walking horse," Sommers said with a faint smile. "We need to find out more about McNeil before we jump to any conclusions."

"Maybe he's one of them Rangers," Jay, the hotel clerk, said. "I heard tell they slip around on the sly sometimes looking into things without advertising who they are."

Sommers ignored him, thinking. "McNeil is down at Kate's place," the rancher said finally. "Cotton, you and Grover mosey down there and get some coffee. Keep an eye on him. Better yet, talk to him."

"What'll we talk to him about?" Rhodes said. "The weather? The cattle market? Birds and the bees? You just tried. Where did it get you?"

"Just strike up a parley with the man and see what more you can learn about what he's doing here, his relationship with Everhart. Do I have to spell everything out for you, Grover?"

"I only thought..."

"Sure, you only thought, Grover. You leave the thinking to me. It's not your strongest feature."

"What do you want me to do, Mr. Sommers?" Jay said.

"What do you do? You wait like the rest of us and keep your ears open. I'm going over to the jail to see Marshal Long. After I find out what McNeil talked to him about, I'll tell him to telegraph the sheriff down at Uvalde asking for everything the law down there knows about him."

Doc Holder took in everything said but contributed nothing to the conversation. When the meeting broke up, Sommers headed for the jail after sending the two cowboys he rode in with back to the ranch. Patrick and Rhodes left for the eating establishment, leaving Doc Holder and Jay alone. Doc returned to the window and peered out. After a while, the hotel clerk broke the brittle silence.

"What do you think, Doc? About what McNeil is up to, I mean."

Without turning from the window, Doc grumbled, "What do I think? Weren't you listening with your good ear when Bull Sommers talked, Jay? He's doing the thinking for all of us. Lord, help us. That's what got us all into this mess to start with."

Chapter 4

Kate's Place

The bell above the door tinkled when McNeil walked in. The place was empty, so he picked a vacant table by the window and sat down. Then, directly, a girl in her twenties with a beautiful face came out of the kitchen. She had her long brown hair gathered into a ponytail at the back of her beautifully shaped head. Her blue eyes inspected McNeil with curiosity. He smiled in response.

"Howdy. What's on the menu?"

"We serve beef and beans for breakfast, beans and beef for lunch, and more beans and beef for supper."

"Then, I guess I'll have beef and beans."

"That's the breakfast menu," the woman said with a grin. "Guess you'll have to come back in the morning unless you're willing to settle for the beans and beef."

McNeil laughed. "Okay, you talked me into it. So beans and beef it is."

"Two bits."

McNeil nodded and fished a twenty-five-cent piece from his pocket. He laid it on the table. The woman scooped up the coin and dropped it into her apron pocket.

"How do you like your beef, mister?"

"Dead and cooked," McNeil said. "I'll take it from there."

The woman smiled before retreating to the kitchen. She was a tall girl with a nice figure. McNeil had little trouble imagining she was a popular item with the local cowhands. Soon the woman returned with a cup and coffee pot. She set the cup in front of McNeil and filled it with the steaming hot black brew.

"Coffee comes with the meal," she said.

"You own this place?"

"Yes, I'm Kate Lamar. I own this eatery, and my brother Jay clerks at the hotel. I expect you're the stranger who arrived today that everyone is flapping their gums about."

"Yeah, I guess the news gets around fast. I'm Pete McNeil."

Kate looked down at him and nodded. "How do you like our mangy, flea-bitten little town so far, Mr. McNeil?"

"Well, I feel like the welcome wagon ran me over," McNeil said. "Seems to me people here don't go out of their way to be friendly. Present company excluded."

"This is a hardscrabble town, Mr. McNeil. People have so little here and scratch for a living. I guess they live with the fear someone might come along and try to take what little they have away. So they are suspicious of strangers."

"The Sommers fellow I met a little while ago seemed prosperous enough."

"Yes, he's the exception. He owns the biggest ranch in this country. And he runs this town.

Bull Sommers came to Texas with the other carpetbaggers after the war. He bought up a lot of grazing land for pennies on the dollar, then brought in the cattle. He's a wealthy man now, the wealthiest around these parts."

Kate returned to the kitchen and then came back with McNeil's beans and beef. Then she refilled his coffee cup.

"Your brother Jay, over at the hotel, told me the town is expecting some cattlemen to arrive any day now. What's that about?"

"The annual cattle drive," Kate said. Since there were no other customers, she pulled a chair out and sat down at the table. "Some fellows from South Texas bring a herd through every year and stop off at Dead Horse Crossing. The local ranchers sell them cattle to round out the herd. Then, the drovers push their cattle on up the Pecos into New Mexico Territory to Raton Pass and around the base of the Rockies to Denver, Colorado."

"The Goodnight-Loving Trail?"

"That's the one. So anyway, the money from the cattle breathes new life into Dead Horse Crossing for another year. If it weren't for the yearly cattle drive, this town would have dried up and blown away with the tumbleweeds years ago."

"Yeah, there are a lot of Texas towns that depend on the cattle drives."

"It's the lifeblood of this town. But, unfortunately, it means we only exist a year at a time."

McNeil nodded.

"How's the steak?"

"Juicy and delicious, just the way I like it."

Kate nodded. "I have one leftover piece of pie in the kitchen if you've got room left for it."

"I've always got room for pie, ma'am."

"You aren't even going to ask what kind of pie?"

McNeil shook his head. "Doesn't matter. All pie is good. Though some pies are better than others."

The bell tinkled when the door opened, and the two cowboys from the hotel, Patrick and Rhodes, walked in.

"Hey Kate, how about some coffee?" Rhodes said, leering at the woman.

"And we'll have pie with the coffee," Patrick added. "We just got paid yesterday."

The two men sat down at a nearby table.

"There's only one piece of pie left," Kate said, getting up.

"Then cut her in half, darlin'," Rhodes said. "We'll share it."

Kate grabbed two cups and the coffee pot and walked to the table occupied by the two cowboys.

"I misspoke," she said, filling the cups. "There was one piece of pie leftover from lunch, but it's spoken for already."

"By him?" Rhodes said, jerking his head toward McNeil.

"You see anyone else in here besides him and you two ornery galoots?"

Kate returned to the counter with the coffee pot and, after setting it down, stayed at the counter instead of returning to McNeil's table. He continued working on the steak and beans, seeming not to notice. But the two cowboys did.

"Hey, Kate," Patrick said. "Since he is getting the pie, I expect he was here sparkin' you before we came in. So go ahead and sit with him. Don't let us crowd your style."

McNeil flushed slightly but said nothing.

"Hey, McNeil," Rhodes said. "That the truth of it? You in here sparkin' our gal, Kate?"

McNeil ignored the remark and continued eating.

"You deaf or just stupid, McNeil," Rhodes taunted. The hefty man pushed back his chair, stood up, and swaggered over to stand beside McNeil's table. "I asked you a question."

McNeil glanced up at Rhodes with undisguised contempt and then cut another piece of steak without offering a reply.

"What's the matter, McNeil? Cat got your tongue?"

McNeil calmly continued eating while ignoring the loud mouth cowboy. Rhodes seemed confused, but his face flushed when Patrick snickered behind him.

"Patrick says you were in the big war," Rhodes said. "You one of them dirty Johnny Rebs?"

McNeil sighed, put his fork down on the plate, and stood up at only an arm's length from Rhodes. Dead silence ensued when Rhodes saw McNeil's gray eyes turn darker and cold. But the cowboy was in too deep now to back up.

"The way I heard it, you Rebs did more running than fighting, and most of y'all got shot in the back."

"You calling me a coward, Rhodes?" McNeil asked in a tone flat and cold as ice water. "If you're joking, better say so now."

Rhodes focused on McNeil's right hand, hovering near the butt of the worn Colt with the bone handles. Rhodes hadn't felt fear since he was a child, but he felt it now. But he saw no way out of the predicament he had foolishly walked into with a man he had badly misjudged.

"I wasn't jokin'," Rhodes stammered.

The chair scraped the floor as Patrick got up from the table behind Rhodes. He slipped to the left to get out of McNeil's line of fire. Patrick held his hands out and above his waist to show he wasn't part of the looming gun play.

"Then, I guess you better back your play, Rhodes," McNeil hissed. "Call the ball."

McNeil was uncomfortably close, and Rhodes knew that he'd still probably get shot even if he got his gun into action first. But what could he do? He went for his gun. Patrick and Kate Lamar saw and would remember what happened next with piercing clarity.

First, McNeil reached out his left hand and grabbed Rhodes' right wrist in a steely grip with the man's gun only half drawn. Then, at the same moment, McNeil raised the Colt in his right hand above his shoulder and slammed the barrel down on Rhodes' head, delivering a vicious blow. It happened so fast that Patrick would say later that he never even saw McNeil's Colt clear the leather. Rhodes sat down like a pole-axed steer and then rolled over onto his face, unconscious. Instinctively, Patrick palmed his six-shooter but paused, staring at the unblinking eye of the muzzle of McNeil's Colt. It looked like the open end of a rain barrel. With deliberate slowness, Patrick took his hand away from his gun and lifted both hands to shoulder level.

"You're smarter than you look, Patrick," McNeil said, twirling the Colt once before dropping it back in the holster. But he held Rhodes' six-shooter in his left hand.

"I'd been within my rights to kill you both," McNeil said. To Patrick, the words sounded like the angry cracks of a bullwhip. "But Miss Lamar saved your worthless hides. I didn't want to get blood all over her clean floor. You must thank her."

Patrick looked at McNeil, dumbfounded.

"Say it," McNeil said. "Thank you, Miss Lamar, for saving our worthless hides."

Patrick's Adam's apple bobbed as he tried to swallow. "Thank you, Miss Lamar, for saving our worthless lives," he stammered.

"Good," McNeil said. "Now, get your companion's carcass out of my sight."

Patrick nodded. He knelt beside Rhodes and rolled the man over on his back. Then, grabbing the unconscious cowboy under the arms, Patrick dragged him toward the door. McNeil stepped to the door and opened it. Patrick backed through it with his burden, and McNeil closed the door behind them.

Looking at the astonished Kate Lamar, McNeil dropped Rhodes' gun on the counter. "You can give it back to him the next time he comes in. And I'm ready for that pie now."

She nodded her head dumbly and left for the kitchen in a daze.

Chapter 5

More Questions Than Answers

BUD LONG WAS STILL sitting in his chair, staring with sightless eyes at the blank wall in front of him, when Bull Sommers entered the jail. Sommers looked from Long to the empty whiskey bottle on the desk, then back at the marshal.

"What did he want?" Sommers demanded. "The stranger. I saw him come in here."

Looking up at Sommers, Long said, "He asked about Denton Everhart and for directions out to the Lazy E. You think he'll cause trouble?"

"Trouble? About what?"

"I don't know," Long said awkwardly. "All I know is I don't want trouble around here. Never again."

"Trouble? You know nothing about Everhart. Do you, Bud?"

"No, I do not. That's the point."

"What you don't know can't hurt you. Can it, Bud?"

"No. I guess not. But maybe there is something I ought to know. Maybe I ought to start asking you some questions before that stranger comes back, breathing down my shirt collar, demanding answers."

"I told you a long time ago. Nothing happened with Everhart you need to worry about, Bud. And in a week, the cattle drive will be here, and we will have put our present difficulties behind us."

"Thing is, I do worry. Maybe I'm not much good at anything else, but I've always been a good worrier." Long paused for a moment. "And I am the law in this town."

"Then, do your job, Bud. Keep it together for another week until this thing blows over."

"What is my job, Mr. Sommers? Maybe you should tell me before McNeil does."

"McNeil will do nothing, and neither will you, Bud."

"Suppose I made up my mind to try."

Sommers glared at Long with menace. "That could be dangerous, Bud. If you bothered to shave once in a while, it would allow you to look in a mirror. Then maybe you would see what I'm looking at right now. It's a little late in the day for you to start thinking you have any authority in this town. So, don't give me that high and mighty talk about being the law in this town."

Long stood up and tried to meet Sommers' withering gaze. But he couldn't, so he dropped back into the chair and lowered his eyes.

"Yes, Mr. Sommers," he said meekly.

"Sommers walked behind the chair and laid a condescending hand on Long's shoulder. Just do what I ask, Bud," he said in a more conciliatory tone. "In a week, this trouble will all be behind us. And I promise you, McNeil won't cause us any trouble. I'll see to it. So you needn't worry."

"Yes, Mr. Sommers." Long said with a sigh.

"Good man," Sommers said. "Now I have a job for you. First, go to Ed Beeson's place and have him open up the post office. Then have him send a wire for you to the sheriff in Uvalde County. Ask him for information about McNeil."

"Like what?"

"I want to know if he's a lawman. One of the boys speculated he might be a Texas Ranger, maybe a federal marshal."

"Well, if he is, and he ain't advertising it, no sheriff will tell us that."

"Maybe not. But if McNeil is an outlaw, that sheriff would tell you that. Wouldn't he? Perhaps the law wants him for something. It could give you an excuse to lock him up. And that would get him out of our hair."

"Okay, I'll send the wire."

"And when you see Beeson, you tell him that if McNeil comes to him about telegraphing anyone, he is not to send any wires. Not under any circumstances. Tell Beeson that's my order. If McNeil asks to send a wire, Beeson is to tell him the wire is down somewhere, and he can't send or receive until a crew makes repairs."

"Yes, Mr. Sommers."

"Let me know when you hear something from Uvalde County."

Without waiting for a reply, Sommers turned and left the jail. Long sighed. Then he got up, put on his hat, and left for Ed Beeson's place.

⸻ ✑ ⸻

Kate Lamar set the generous slice of pie on the table before McNeil. Then she refilled his coffee cup and poured herself a cup before sitting down at the table. Kate lifted her cup to drink, but her hand shook so badly she sloshed coffee onto the red and white checkered tablecloth. So, she set the cup back down. McNeil pretended not to notice, lifting a fork full of apple pie to his mouth. Then, after chewing and swallowing, he looked at Kate and smiled.

"That's some of the best apple pie I've had in a while."

Kate, searching for words to say, barely registered the compliment. Finally, she spoke.

"I've never seen anything like that."

"I'm sorry you had to see it and sorry for bringing trouble to your door."

"I admire you didn't kill those two hotheads," Kate said. "As you said, you had every right. No one could have faulted you if you had. It would have been a fair shooting if there ever was one. But those two are still more boys than men. They are young and reckless and very proud."

McNeil looked thoughtful as he chewed another fork full of pie. Then, after swallowing, he said, "The graveyards are full of men who were young, reckless, and very proud."

Kate nodded somberly. "It scared Grover to death when he realized he'd gone too far. But then, he couldn't figure a way out without looking like a coward. He's lucky you let him off with a bump on the head. And then, I thought Cotton was going to draw on you. They came in here hunting trouble and bit off more than they could chew."

McNeil shrugged and grinned and then finished up his pie. Kate Lamar studied him as he ate. There was something about the man, an air of monumental dependability and quiet humor. But in his eyes earlier, she had seen a man who was no stranger to violence. She didn't doubt he had killed men before.

"You think the trouble is over?" Kate said.

"I think those two cowboys will pull their horns in for a while," McNeil said. "But as you said, they're proud, and I shamed them both. So I expect I haven't seen the last of them. But I doubt they will behave as recklessly the next time. It would probably have been to my advantage to have killed them both and been done with it."

"Then why didn't you?"

"As I said, I didn't want to cause you inconvenience by getting blood all over your clean floor."

McNeil's gray eyes twinkled, and Kate couldn't tell whether he was serious or joking. Not until the man laughed. But then he turned somber. "There is no pleasure in killing a man, Kate. But sometimes, a man gives you no other choice in the matter."

"I suppose."

"Your brother said the cattlemen are due any day. He's in a big hurry to push me out of my room."

"Oh, I don't expect them until late next week if they stick to their usual schedule. And the trail boss will send a wire when they are two or three days out. But, as far as I know, he has sent no wire yet. So I don't see why Jay is pestering you."

"Can I ask you something, Kate?"

"Sure, but I can't promise I'll answer. It depends on what it is."

McNeil chuckled. "Fair enough. But don't worry. It's nothing of a personal nature."

"Then ask away."

"Do you know Denton Everhart?"

Kate looked down and said nothing for several moments. Then, without meeting McNeil's gaze, she answered. "I knew Denton. He was a fine man."

"So, he's truly dead."

"Yes."

"Why do I get the impression no one in town wants to talk to me about him?"

McNeil got the same impression about Kate Lamar but left it unsaid.

"I don't rightly know," she said in almost a whisper, still avoiding his gaze.

McNeil recognized Kate Lamar wasn't an accomplished liar. She either didn't wish to talk about Denton Everhart for some reason, or maybe it frightened her. Maybe someone had ordered her to keep her mouth shut. So McNeil chose not to press the issue.

"Can you tell me how to get to his ranch from town? I'd like to take a ride out there."

"I wouldn't do that," Kate said, with no explanation.

"Still, I'd like to see Everhart's spread."

"To what purpose?" Kate asked with surprising vehemence. "Who was Denton Everhart to you?"

"We served together in the army during the war. Denton saved my life once at a place called Antietam. We became friends and have remained close friends since."

"So, you came here to visit him?"

"In a manner of speaking. It's been almost three years since I last saw Denton. I know his younger sister, Nancy. She came to see me a week ago. Nancy said Denton wrote to her every week, like clockwork. But she hadn't received a letter from him in over a month. She was concerned."

"Maybe he was busy with the ranch and hadn't time to write."

"Nancy didn't think that was the case. And in the last letter Denton wrote to her, he mentioned having some difficulties here. But he didn't offer any details about the nature of the troubles. I guess he didn't want to worry her unduly."

"I see."

"Anyway, I was preparing to leave for Denver, so I told Nancy I'd stop here and check on her brother on the way. So, that's why I'm here in Dead Horse Crossing."

"Well, sadly, you will now become the bearer of bad news for her. Denton must have passed soon after writing that last letter."

"So, he died a month ago?"

"About that, yes."

McNeil didn't tell her that Sommers told him that Denton had died six months ago. The large time discrepancy seemed curious. It was one more reason he believed the town was hiding something. Now he suspected it had something to do with Denton Everhart.

"I find it curious that no one here attempted to notify Denton's next of kin."

"Perhaps no knew he had any," Kate said. "I sure didn't until you told me."

"Well, now that you know the whole story, will you give me directions to the Lazy E? There might be some keepsake at the ranch house Nancy would take comfort in getting."

Kate shook her head. "I doubt it, Pete."

"Still, I'm here. It won't hurt anything to look. So, how about the directions to the Lazy E?"

Kate seemed almost panic-stricken. "Pete, you seem like a good man. Please don't ask me. You shouldn't go out there."

"Why?"

"Bull Sommers wouldn't like it. He may already give you trouble when he finds out what happened here today. He won't take kindly to your rude treatment of his men, no matter how much they had it coming. Bull Sommers will take it as a personal affront."

McNeil stood up. He reached into his pocket and then slammed another two-bit coin on the table.

"That's for the pie," he said coldly. "I'll ride the country hereabouts until I find the Lazy E on my own. I'm tired of asking for help from the inhospitable people of this town. Can't say I've never met a bunch of unfriendlier folks in my life."

Kate stood with slumped shoulders, hanging her head low. Then, without looking McNeil in the eye, she said, "Take the main road three miles north out of town. The road makes a sharp bend east there. After the bend, the first trail running north will take you to the Lazy E. After about a mile, you'll see the ranch."

"Thanks," McNeil said with more sharpness than he had intended. He turned and walked to the door."

"Pete," Kate said.

McNeil paused with his hand on the door and looked back over his shoulder.

"Yes?"

"I'm sorry about your friend," Kate said. "Truly, I am. But please remember what I told you about how important the annual trail drive is to the people of this town. Haven't you ever felt desperate, Pete? When folks are desperate and feel threatened—when they feel their livelihoods and survival itself are at stake, they will do anything to remove the threat. They rationalize doing things they may never have imagined ever doing."

"What are you trying to say, Kate?"

"Nothing. I've already said too much. You would be wise, Pete, if you climbed on your horse tomorrow morning and left this town. I wish you would. For your sake. I don't wish to see you come to any grief."

"Thanks for the heartfelt concern and the advice," McNeil said with sarcasm. Then he opened the door and went out, feeling deeply troubled. The people of Dead Horse Crossing were hiding something and McNeil was now determined to find out what it was.

Chapter 6

Suspicions Mount

MCNEIL TOOK A WALK to the town's cemetery at the edge of town. Out on the dismal plain, the graveyard looked forlorn and forgotten. Hanging from the crossbar of the two posts marking the entrance was a wooden sign in an extreme state of dilapidation. Blistered by the relentless sun and weathered by the elements, the dry-rotted sign hung irregularly because of one of the rusty wires holding it to the crossbar being longer than the other. Flaking paint lettering identified the site: Horse Head Crossing Town Cemetery. On either side of the graveyard, the ocean-like desert plains stretched into infinity. McNeil removed his hat and wiped the sweat from his forehead with a bandana. The late afternoon sun on the horizon lay over the desert wasteland like a gigantic red bruise from which heatwaves radiated out over the dust-choked land. Replacing his hat, McNeil walked through the open entrance. The cemetery and the terrain surrounding it had, if nothing else, the quality of inertia and immutability. Nothing stirred, not even the wind—nothing moved, not even an insect.

Graveyard and terrain were trapped, caught forever in the sullen, abrasive desert environment.

McNeil spied an aged cowboy kneeling beside a grave marker holding his weather-beaten hat by the brim. He walked over to the man, who looked up when he heard McNeil's boots crunching on the dirt. The older man stood and blinked at McNeil with watery eyes.

"Howdy, old-timer," McNeil said. "Did you know Denton Everhart?"

The old cowboy smiled, revealing yellowed teeth. "Oh, I know most all these folks," he said, sweeping his arm in an arc that encompassed the cemetery in its entirety. "This is where my wife rests, and where all my friends are."

"But what about Denton Everhart?"

The man nodded his head. "There's a marker right over there with his name on it. I'll show you, youngster."

"Much obliged," McNeil said and followed the man to another grave site.

"Here it is," the man said, pointing at a simple wooden cross set into the dirt. "When I got here today, it was here. But it wasn't when I was here last week."

McNeil looked at the marker. Someone had carved on the crossbar: DENTON EVERHART 1840 -1881. First, Sommers had told McNeil that Denton Everhart had been dead for six months. Then Kate Lamar told him his friend had died a month ago. But looking at the mounded earth, McNeil knew they had both lied. While he knew the Llano Estacado received infrequent rainfall, there could be no mistake that someone had dug and filled the grave he looked at not more than a week before.

"Thanks, old-timer," McNeil said. Then he turned and walked back to the hotel.

When McNeil entered the hotel lobby, he found there only Jay Lamar, the hotel clerk, and the older derby-wearing gent that he'd seen loafing in the lobby before. McNeil heard Jay call the man Doc just before they suddenly left off talking when he walked through the door. McNeil approached the man.

"Are you the town doctor?"

"Yes, I'm Doc Holder," the man said, looking ill at ease. "Are you in need of a doctor?"

"No. I need answers to a couple of questions. First, Bull Sommers told me that Denton Everhart died six months ago of cholera. Is that true? And did you tend to him when he got sick?"

Holder shifted uncomfortably and glanced at Jay Lamar and back at McNeil. "That's right. Denton took bad sick with cholera. But there was nothing I could do for him."

"When did he die, exactly?"

"I don't give out information on my patients, even after they're deceased, to just anybody who happens to walk in."

"Is the date of Everhart's funeral and burial also secret information?"

"Talk to the undertaker."

"Information is tough to come by around here. I can't seem to get any answers."

"Maybe you should talk to the marshal."

The hint of a smile appeared on McNeil's lips. "I tried that. The marshal wouldn't even admit he knew Denton Everhart."

"Well, Mr. McNeil, I can't help you then."

"What's this town hiding, doctor? What are you people covering up?"

"I'm sure I do not know what you're talking about."

Jay Lamar walked up to stand beside Holder. "Where do you get off interrogating the folks in this town, mister?" he said. "You aren't from around here. You have no right. For someone who asks a lot of questions, you don't talk much about yourself."

"I'm not curious about me."

"Well, folks around here would like to know what you're doing in Dead Horse Crossing. We're all real curious about that."

Holder interrupted. "If you gentlemen will excuse me, I have to go check on a patient. I have a man in my surgery with a serious head injury."

"That's another thing," Lamar said, pointing his finger at McNeil. "You might have killed Grover Rhodes, hitting him over the head like that. And for no reason. I don't know why the marshal hasn't already arrested you."

"For a man who runs his mouth mighty loose, you don't seem to have the facts, Lamar," McNeil retorted. "Rapping a surly cowboy on the head when he tried to draw on me doesn't seem like much a crime. He's darn lucky all he got was a bump on the head instead of a good dose of lead. Maybe you should ask your sister what happened over at her place before running your mouth."

Holder eased toward the front door, and the hotel clerk retreated behind the front desk. McNeil shook his head in disgust and then turned and climbed the steps to his room. He didn't like this town. He didn't like the people who lived in it. But he wasn't leaving until he found out what had happened to his friend.

Chapter 7

Decision Time

THE FOLLOWING MORNING, ED Beeson, local postmaster and operator of the postal telegraph, sat at his desk sorting mail. The telegraph started clicking. Beeson keyed a response and put on his spectacles. Then he grabbed a pad and pencil. He listened and scribbled as the message came through from Uvalde. The telegraph stopped as suddenly as it had started. He read the message he had copied again and gulped nervously, a confused look on his face. Then he took off the spectacles, jumped up, and hurried out his office door.

Beeson was rushing toward the jail when he noticed Marshal Long was standing on the boardwalk outside the hotel with a group of other men. He made an immediate course correction and headed for the hotel. Drawing closer, Beeson saw Bull Sommers, Jay Lamar, Doc Holder, Patrick, and Rhodes were in the group outside the hotel with Bud Long. He saw that a white bandage swathed Rhodes' head.

"I want you to arrest him, Marshal," Sommers said flatly. "He attacked and injured one of my hands. McNeil might have killed him."

"I already talked to Kate," Long said, almost as if apologizing. "She saw the whole thing. Kate says Grover provoked him and was lucky McNeil didn't kill him."

"Patrick and Grover will testify against him," Sommers countered. "It will be their word against hers. You know how excited women get in situations like that. The woman probably doesn't even have a clear recollection of what happened."

Patrick took the last drag from his smoke and flicked the butt into the street. "Guess you better count me out of that deal," he drawled. "I'm not lying about the man."

"What's that, Patrick?" Sommers said sharply. "You going soft on me? When a man works for me, I expect him to ride for the brand."

"I ride for the brand, boss. Won't any man dare say different that wants to keep on breathing. But there are two things I won't do for money. I won't lie for it, and I won't kill for it. After that, I'm pretty much open to anything. After Grover pushed him too hard, McNeil could have killed old Grover and me besides. And no one could have said squat about it. But he didn't. And I, for one, am grateful."

Red-faced, Sommers was about to reply when Beeson ran up the steps with a hobnailed clatter onto the boardwalk and then paused for a moment to catch his breath.

"I got your reply here, Marshal," Beeson said, waving the paper in his hand.

"From Uvalde County?" Long said, reaching for the paper.

"Yes, Marshal," Beeson said. He'd barely got the words out before Sommers had snatched the telegram from his hand.

"What does it say?" Jay said, as Sommers read the message. "Who is that fella McNeil, anyway?"

When Sommers said nothing, Beeson exclaimed, "The sheriff in Uvalde County never heard of him. That's what it says. He asked around down there and couldn't find anyone who knew McNeil or anything about him. Nothing."

"Where does that leave us?" Jay said.

Doc Holder said, "I'll tell you where…"

"Shut up!" Sommers exclaimed.

He folded the telegram and put it into his pocket. Then he took Patrick and Rhodes by the arm and guided them down the steps to the street. The three men kept walking until they were out of earshot of those they left behind on the boardwalk.

Sommers said, "Now, Grover…"

"I think McNeil is nothing, boss," Rhodes interrupted. "A nobody."

"Is he?" Sommers said.

Grover nodded. "So, there's nothing to worry about, boss. I think he'll pull stakes any time now and ride out of here."

"Will he? You've really got the brains, Grover. Don't you?"

"I don't know who he is or whether he's the law," Patrick said. "But he sure ain't a nobody. McNeil is a sure enough gunman, the real deal. And that's a fact. I never saw a man pull iron so fast. Fact is, I didn't see it. That Colt was in the holster one second. The next, he was clubbing Grover here on the skull with it. He could have emptied it in Grover and reloaded before Grover even knew he was dead."

Rhodes looked at Patrick with irritation. "You could have backed my play."

"And got killed right along with you, you ignorant wretch? Mrs. Patrick raised no foolish children.

Unlike you, I'm smart enough not to grab a catamount by the tail."

"Knock off the bickering," Sommers commanded.

"I still say there is no reason to worry," Rhodes said. "What can he find out? That Everhart was…" Rhodes stopped talking when Sommers glared at him.

"Suppose he finds out? Suppose he finds it all out?"

Rhodes shrugged. Patrick stood listening with a bemused expression.

"A man like McNeil could cause some pretty big problems," Sommers said. "But who would miss McNeil if he just, say, disappeared? Who?" Sommers looked from Patrick to Rhodes to Patrick.

Rhodes broke eye contact with Sommers, looked at the ground, and shuffled his feet. He felt uneasy as he considered Sommers' meaning and the risks of taking on a man like McNeil would entail for him in particular. He still recalled the fear that gripped him when he had last looked into those dead gray eyes.

"Grover!" Sommers exclaimed in exasperation.

"Huh?"

"Why don't we wait?" Patrick said.

Sommers turned to regard him. "Wait for what?"

"I mean, leave him be, and maybe he'll ride on out of here. He won't find out anything. How could he? No one is telling him squat. All of us in this town have too much at stake to wag our tongues to a stranger. We still have at least three days before that herd shows up. I think he'll go before then."

"Not a man like McNeil," Sommers said. "I think he's suspicious already, and he won't go until he finds out what's going on here. Men like him are do-gooders and trouble makers. And if he figures it all out, you can bet he will ruin things for all of us."

"But there's no danger yet. So I'm saying we shouldn't go off half-cocked. Let's wait and see."

Sommers turned and appealed to Rhodes. "No danger, he says. McNeil is like a carrier of smallpox. There's been a fever running through this town since he arrived. If we don't act, the infection will only spread."

"If McNeil rides out to the Lazy E, he'll figure it out," Rhodes agreed. "The boys have at least two more days' work to finish up out there."

"That's what I mean," Sommers said. "That's why we have to address this now. Of course, if you want to take a chance..."

"Not me," Rhodes said firmly. "Too much is riding on this."

Sommers looked at Patrick, but the young cowboy said nothing.

Sommers looked back at Rhodes. "All right then..."

"It's not all right," Patrick exclaimed. "You're so almighty quick to kill, but he's a man, not an animal. And after what I've seen, I expect you jawing about it is a mite easier than doing it."

Sommers looked from Patrick to Rhodes. "Well, just listen to him, would you?" Sommers sneered. Then he whirled back to Patrick. "All this sniveling might make someone think you're losing your nerve, Patrick. I'm trying to save all our necks. If I don't, who will?"

Patrick replied, "All I said was..."

"Who will?" Sommers demanded. "You, Patrick? Doc? That drunk Bud Long? Jay Lamar or his idiot sister? Who?"

Patrick withered under Sommers' angry scowl and kept silent.

"Maybe you're ready to turn tail and run away," Sommers said.

There was a long silence.

"It's too late for that," Rhodes said, eyeing Patrick. "He's in this, and he ain't running no place."

"All right then," Sommers said. "It's settled. Now, we work out the plan and take care of the problem."

Chapter 8

A Turn for the Worse

WHEN MCNEIL WENT DOWNSTAIRS, the lobby was empty. Even the hotel clerk was absent. He stepped outside onto the boardwalk and saw Sommers and the two cowboys huddled together, having a pow-wow. They paid him no mind, so he returned the favor. He turned and walked the other direction toward Kate's place.

Townsfolk crowded the eatery this time, but McNeil found an empty table at the back and sat down. After he walked in, the conversation had gone quiet, and no one made eye contact with him. Finally, Kate came over, took his order, and filled his coffee cup, but didn't stay around for small talk. Since it was the breakfast hour, McNeil had gone for the beef and beans this time. He hankered for a proper breakfast like his mother used to serve—eggs, a thick slice of smoked ham, and plenty of biscuits and gravy. The fare at Kate's place was tasty and filling. But it reminded him too much of all the meals he'd eaten on the many cattle drives from chuck wagons over the years.

Kate served him his plate of food, refilled his coffee, and hurried away. McNeil ate his breakfast in silence. He contemplated apologizing to her, but that would have to wait until later. McNeil wasn't about to humble himself in front of a crowd of townsfolk. When he finished, he left his money on the table for the meal and went out.

McNeil walked to the livery to get his horse. He figured it was time to ride out to the Lazy E and see what he might learn. It seemed clear there were people in town who didn't want him to visit the ranch, which naturally made McNeil curious to know why. Was his friend's ranch part of the big secret?

He found the livery stable locked up when he arrived, and no one was around. McNeil pulled his watch from his vest pocket and saw it was after nine. He'd never known of a livery stable being closed at nine o'clock in the morning on a weekday. McNeil sat down on an overturned wooden bucket to await the liveryman's return. Near ten, the liveryman had still not shown up, and McNeil was out of patience. Casting about, he found a pitchfork leaning against an outside wall of the stable next to the corral. He carried the pitchfork to the front, inserted a steel point between the hasp and the door, and yanked hard on the handle. The hasp pulled away easily from the weathered wood door. McNeil opened the door, went inside, and saddled his roan.

McNeil found a pencil and paper on a table near the front doors on the way out. He scribbled a note to the liveryman, explaining he'd needed his horse and would pay for the damages he'd done when he returned to town later. Then McNeil climbed aboard the roan and headed north out of town on the main road. In less than an hour, he came to the curve Kate Lamar had described and, after rounding it, found the trail heading north to the ranch. McNeil saw tendrils of black smoke curling into the sky up ahead. Then, a little further along, he smelled the aroma of cooking meat. It reminded him of the smells of the many after roundup barbecues he'd attended in the past.

McNeil had given his horse its head when he rode out of town since he was in no hurry. And the gelding continued plodding along at the animal's preferred pace, an easy walk. Finally, about fifteen minutes after leaving the main road, horse and rider topped a small rise, and the Lazy E ranch came into McNeil's view. What he saw was not what he had expected. McNeil reined up and dismounted when he reached the post and rail fencing enclosing the ranch yard. He looped the reins over a fence rail and then leaned on the fence and surveyed what remained of his friend's former home. The ranch house had burned to the ground, leaving behind a twisted, blackened pile of burned timbers. Only the stone chimney still stood, and it was black with soot. Was this what Kate Lamar had meant when she'd told him she doubted he'd find any keepsakes to take back to Denton Everhart's sister?

McNeil sensed the anger growing within him, anger as hot as the fire that had consumed the ruined ranch house. How could Kate not have told him what he'd find here? Was the woman that unfeeling? At that moment, McNeil no longer disliked the people of Dead Horse Crossing. He hated them. He hated them all. Before, he might have settled for finding out what misfortune had befallen his friend Denton so that he could explain it to Nancy. But not anymore. Looking at the burned-out remains of the ranch house, McNeil resolved he wouldn't leave this miserable town until he uncovered the dirty secret the townspeople were protecting. Before he called it quits, McNeil planned to spread a little ruin of his own.

The sound of approaching hoof beats shook McNeil from his dark thoughts. He turned to see four horsemen approaching at a gallop. He recognized them—Marshal Bud Long, Bull Sommers, and his two cowboys, Patrick and Rhodes. The men pulled up in a cloud of dust. The marshal, Sommers, and Rhodes stepped down from their saddles, but Patrick stayed on his horse. Both Sommers and Rhodes levered the Winchesters they held and pointed them at McNeil. The marshal had the scattergun under his arm but held the muzzle pointed at the ground. Long looked like a different man. He was clean-shaven and had on a clean broadcloth shirt. It appeared the man had even shined the tin star pinned on his chest. Sommers and Rhodes also wore badges. McNeil looked up at Patrick, who looked as if he wished he were some place else. Anywhere else. The man refused even to meet his gaze.

"What's this about, Marshal?" McNeil said.

"I'm placing you under arrest, Mr. McNeil," Long said. "Please hand me that pistol, the butt first. We want no trouble."

"On what charge?" McNeil said, unable to hide his astonishment.

"Suspicion of breaking and entering."

"No suspicion about it," Sommers crowed. "Witnesses saw you breaking into the livery stable in town."

"Marshal, I can explain that. I needed my horse, and there was no one at the livery. I waited for an hour, but the liveryman never showed. So, I let myself in to get my horse. And I left a note for the liveryman explaining the damage, and I plan to pay him for the repairs."

"None of that matters, McNeil," Sommers said. "You broke the law. Old Sam woke up ill and wasn't able to open up today. It would have been best if you had waited until Sam arranged for a temporary replacement."

"You needed to get up a posse for such a minor matter, Marshal?" McNeil chided.

"That's my business, Mr. McNeil. Now hand over that pistol. I won't ask again."

Gingerly, McNeil lifted the Colt from the holster using only his thumb and forefinger. He felt that Sommers and Rhodes were itching to pull the triggers of their rifles and hoping for an excuse. Patrick continued to sit his horse with his hands stacked on the saddle horn. He hadn't even drawn his pistol, nor was he wearing a badge. Did the man disapprove of what was happening?

"On your word that you will remain cooperative, I won't tie your hands, Mr. McNeil," Long said.

"You have it, Marshal. I'm for law and order all the way. That's why you didn't need a posse. I would not resist an officer of the law."

"Good to hear, Mr. McNeil. Then fork your horse, and we'll return to town."

"Whatever you say, Marshal."

McNeil climbed aboard the roan, and the other men mounted. McNeil and Long took the lead, riding side by side, and the others brought up the rear.

"Marshal, you mind telling me what happened to Denton Everhart's house?"

"I don't rightly know, Mr.McNeil, as I didn't know it had burned until just now. I haven't been out this way in a long while."

For once, McNeil thought the lawman was telling the truth.

"So, once we get back to town, how do we get this misunderstanding settled?"

"You will remain in jail until the circuit judge arrives in about a week. Then he'll hold your trial?"

"You plan to keep me in jail for a week?"

"I'm afraid so, Mr. McNeil. That's just how it works."

"But I didn't break into the livery for any nefarious purpose. I stole nothing, and the damage was minimal. Also, I told you I left a note and intended to pay for the repairs."

"You must wait to plead your case to the judge."

"That's enough talking, McNeil," Sommers said from behind. "You're a prisoner. You don't speak until spoken to from here on out."

McNeil stared straight ahead, not even acknowledging the pompous windbag. But he held his peace the rest of the way to town. Mostly because his mind was working to figure out what this farce was all about. By the time they reached the town, he felt sure he knew. Disarmed and locked in a jail cell made McNeil an easy target for anyone who might wish him harm. McNeil knew he couldn't remain in jail long. He wouldn't last a week waiting on a judge. He'd be dead long before the judge arrived. It wasn't difficult to figure out. First, the people of the town wanted him gone. Now they intended to prevent him from ever leaving.

Chapter 9

Jailed

EACH DAY HAD PASSED much the same as the day before during McNeil's first two days in the town's jail. The marshal had guarded him from sunup until Patrick relieved him at around four in the afternoon. Patrick stayed until Rhodes came on duty an hour before midnight, and Rhodes stayed until the marshal came back on duty in the mornings. Kate Lamar brought meals over from her place for both the guards and the prisoner. His first night on duty, Rhodes had stood outside the cell gloating and told McNeil he would shoot him dead if he tried to break jail. McNeil figured that was their plan. They would kill him in the cell and then justify it by claiming he had tried to escape.

But, of course, there wasn't much chance he could escape even if you wanted to try. The only time the marshal or his irregular deputies opened the cell door was when Kate brought the meals to the jail. Then, after unlocking the cell door, the guard stood outside the cell with his pistol drawn while Kate stepped into the doorway and handed McNeil his plate of beef and beans. Kate never spoke to him. She only handed over the plate and a spoon, looked at him with sadness, and then left. Afterward, the guard locked the cell door and left McNeil alone until the time of the next meal serving.

McNeil figured he hadn't much time left. He felt sure Sommers had no intention of letting him live to see a judge. But with no hope of escaping his confinement, there was little to do about it. He had taken the precaution of moving the bunk beneath the small barred cell window. That protected him from someone on horseback shooting him through the bars over the window like a fish in a barrel.

Laying on his back on the bunk, McNeil stared at the ceiling illuminated only by the moonlight coming through the small window, contemplating his predicament. He figured it must be going on one o'clock in the morning, since Rhodes had relieved Patrick some time ago. Then his thoughts turned to Patrick.

McNeil couldn't quite figure out the man. He'd seemed eager enough to try and put the run on McNeil that day he had checked into the hotel. But the man's demeanor had changed since then. Patrick seemed almost shamed by McNeil's recent treatment, as if he wasn't in agreement with Sommers' plan. At mealtimes, Patrick was the only one who didn't hold a gun on him while Kate served the grub. And Patrick never made eye contact with him.

Thoughts of Everhart and the Lazy E came to mind. McNeil now felt certain Denton's ranch was the key to whatever affair the townsfolk were covering up. Who had burned Denton's ranch house, and why? What had the smoke and smell of cooking meat been about? Then, suddenly, something with a little heft to it tumbled out of the window above his bunk and landed on the coarse wool blanket pulled up to McNeil's chest. He groped for the object. Finding it, he took hold of it and held it up to the moonlight. It was a large brass key, the key to the cell door.

Was someone trying to help him? If so, who? And why? Or was this part of the plan? Had someone supplied him with a key so that Rhodes could shoot him dead, claiming he had tried to escape? McNeil didn't know the answer. But he knew one thing. Someone had given him the only chance he had to escape certain death.

Rhodes always left the wooden door ajar that separated the marshal's office from the cell block. During the nights, McNeil had awakened to the sounds of Rhodes' snores. He resolved to stay awake this night and would make his move after the snoring started.

Hours later, McNeil finally heard Rhodes snoring. Quietly, he threw off the blanket and got up from the bunk. He crept to the cell door. First, using spit, he lubricated the iron hinges, knowing they squeaked something fierce whenever the door opened. Then, reaching through the bars, McNeil slid the key into the door lock and turned it. Next, he eased the door open, only wide enough to allow him to slip through sideways. Then, silently, he stole to the wooden door. Because the door opened outward, McNeil could peer through the crack between the door and frame and see Rhodes sitting in the chair behind the desk. The man's feet were on the desk. He had reared back in the chair and gone to sleep with his hat pulled down over his face.

After pushing the door open with care, McNeil crept on cat's feet toward the sleeping cowboy. At Rhodes' side, McNeil balled his right fist and punched the sleeping man square in the jaw right in front of the ear. Rhodes' hat flew off, and the man lay still, slumped in the chair with his head lolled to the side. Instead of sleeping, Rhodes now reclined unconscious in the chair. Like most men of Irish descent, McNeil had taken up fighting in his youth. He had even trained as a boxer as a teenager before heading west. While he had long since abandoned the Queensbury rules, McNeil knew how to throw a punch. And being struck by McNeil was akin to being kicked by a mule.

After easing Rhodes to the floor, McNeil dragged the man into the jail cell. There, he first stripped Rhodes of his gun belt. Next, he unfastened and pulled the belt from the man's pants. Then, rolling Rhodes onto his belly, McNeil bound his wrists with the leather belt. Finally, he unknotted the cowboy's bandana, removed it from his neck, and tied it over Rhodes' mouth as a gag.

Picking up the gun belt, McNeil exited the cell and locked the door. Then, back in the marshal's office, he closed and barred the wooden door. That would keep Rhodes occupied until the marshal returned a few hours later.

Opening the front door, McNeil checked the street outside. Nothing stirred at the early morning hour. Rhodes had left his pony tied to the hitching rail out front, and the saddle and blanket draped over the rail. Instead of making his way to the livery for his roan, McNeil saddled Rhodes' horse to save time. Then he went back into the jail for his Colt. But after rummaging through the marshal's desk,

McNeil failed to find his gun belt. Someone had taken it.

He couldn't get at the long guns in the rack, which the marshal had secured with an iron bar and a heavy padlock. Pulling Rhodes' pistol from the holster, McNeil saw it was a newer model of his Colt. He opened the cylinder gate, eased back the hammer a little, and rotated the cylinder. Finding the handgun fully loaded, he closed the gate and stuck the pistol into the belt of his pants. Rhodes' gun belt was too big for him and useless. After thumbing extra cartridges from the loops of the gun belt, McNeil put them into his pocket. Then, he left the jail.

Outside, McNeil put a foot in the stirrup and climbed into the saddle. He walked the cow pony to the edge of town and then spurred the dun into a gallop. He wanted to get to the Lazy E before daybreak.

Chapter 10

The Secret Exposed

At the Lazy E, McNeil found concealment in a thicket of honey mesquite interspersed with thorny shrubs and creosote bush back of the ruined ranch house. As the sky grew lighter, he scanned the arid grasslands from his hiding spot. Dead, bloated cattle lay scattered about on the short grass.

Three cowboys rode over a knoll and headed for the dead cattle about an hour after daybreak. After pulling their kerchiefs up over their noses and mouths, they unlimbered their lariats and began casting loops onto the hind legs of the beeves. Then they dallied the ropes around their saddle horns and dragged the carcasses away to what appeared a distant arroyo. Horses, riders, and carcasses disappeared over the lip of the deep-sided gully. Moments later, the cowpunchers and their mounts reappeared. The men looped their ropes for another cast as they walked the horses toward the dead animals littering the landscape. Finally, the sinister truth the townspeople were concealing became clear.

Suddenly, McNeil's borrowed horse, aware of the presence of the other horses, whinnied a greeting. The three cowboys froze and craned their necks to look in McNeil's direction in unison. He hurriedly crawled to the horse to put a hand over its muzzle to prevent further neighing. But his sudden movement startled the dun. The animal reared, snapping the shrub branch McNeil had tied the reins to, and then the horse wheeled and galloped from the thicket, stirrups slapping its sides. When the ranch hands saw the horse, they immediately wheeled their mounts and rode toward the thicket.

The copse offered concealment but no cover. So, McNeil got up and burst from the thicket out the backside. He spied a pile of boulders on the rise about a hundred yards ahead and made for them at a sprint. He could fort up there and hold off the cowmen. Looking back over his shoulder, he saw the three riders closing the distance with whoops, hollers, and loops twirling above their heads. Then, on the wind, he caught the shout of one of them.

"Rope him and drag him. Make it look like an accident."

Though swift of foot, McNeil was no match for the speed of the cow ponies. So, while running, he pulled the Colt from his belt, pointed it behind him beneath his armpit, and fired several shots. He did not expect to hit the riders, nor did he want to. McNeil didn't wish to kill indiscriminately if he could avoid it. He only hoped to discourage his pursuers.

The mounted men slowed in response to the gunfire. But they came on after discarding their ropes and pulling their pistols. Soon bullets buzzed past McNeil. The riders were almost upon him, and the boulders were still forty or fifty yards away. When the running man felt a bullet snatch at the side of his shirt, he stopped and turned. Then, with the bullets whizzing past him like angry bees, McNeil stood tall in the storm of lead, took careful aim at the closest cowhand, and fired. The man tumbled backward from the saddle and hit the ground. The other two men reined up abruptly and wheeled their horses. Then they galloped back to the side of their fallen companion. One man jumped from his horse and went to his downed pardner's side. The other continued banging away at McNeil as he turned and broke into a zig-zag run for the rocky rise.

McNeil reached the first boulder just as a bullet struck it and ricocheted with an ominous whine. Then he felt a burning on the side of his head. He had no sooner put a hand to his head and registered the sticky wetness than he dropped to the ground, unconscious.

McNeil awakened to the sound of voices, his head throbbing. His eyes fluttered open but refused to focus. And he felt sick to his stomach.

"You think I killed him?" someone said.

"Not outright. He's still breathing. But you got him. There's a lump the size of a hen's egg on the side of his skull."

"So, do we finish him off or what?"

"No," said a third speaker through gritted teeth.

"Why not, Chick? He shot you, tried to kill you."

"He wasn't aiming to kill me. Any man can hit a rider on horseback at full gallop with a pistol knows a thing or two about shootin'. He shot me through the shoulder on purpose."

"How you feeling, Chick?"

"I'm okay. The fall hurt worse than the bullet. It knocked the wind out of me a little and might have cracked a rib or two."

"Y'all ever seen this feller before?"

"No, but I know it's that stranger everyone is going on about in town. They said at breakfast this morning he broke jail after knocking old Grover into next Sunday again afore he stole his horse and pistol."

"Well, tarnation, if we ain't goin' to kill him, what are we doin' with him?"

"Jimbo, go catch up Rhodes' pony. Slim, you fetch some piggin' strings. Then, we'll tie his hands afore he comes around, put him aboard the pony, and haul him into town."

"Sounds like a plan, Chick. I'm glad to get a break from draggin' and burnin' these darned old dead cows. The smell gets worse by the day."

"Well, being shot up, I guess I'm done with that now. But old man Sommers will send you boys right back out here after we get this feller into town. That herd will be here in another two or three days. You have to finish the job before then."

McNeil felt the men pick him up and hoist him onto a saddle a while later.

"He's in bad shape. Better tie him in the saddle, or we'll be stoppin' and pickin' him up all the way back to town."

Tied to the saddle was okay by McNeil. Unfortunately, his eyes still wouldn't focus properly, and the world was in a dead spin. He had wretched right after they threw him onto the horse. So, at least his roiling belly felt somewhat better.

After securing him to the saddle, the three cowboys climbed on their horses. And then they turned their ponies and rode toward Dead Horse Crossing with one leading McNeil's mount.

Chapter 11

Getting Doped

MᴄNᴇɪʟ ᴡᴀs ɪɴ ᴀɴᴅ out of consciousness on the ride back to town. When he next woke, he lay on a soft bed and heard men talking in the room. Hoping to learn something, McNeil lay quiet and still. He recognized the voices.

"I don't understand why you're treating him, Doc," Sommers said.

"Because I took an oath to do no harm, that's why."

"I'm only saying, if he dies of natural causes, it solves our problem, and our hands stay clean."

"The wound wouldn't have proved fatal anyway unless an infection set in. I only removed a sliver of a bullet from the wound. He must have caught a ricochet, and the fragment didn't penetrate his skull. I'm no criminal. Withholding care would have only caused this man to suffer needlessly. And that would be criminal."

"Okay, Doc. I get it. Get off your high horse."

"I need some help with this man. How about Kate?"

"All right, Doc. Jay, fetch your sister. Tell her Doc needs her here, so her helper will have to run her place for a while. At least until McNeil is well enough for us to put him back in jail."

"Okay, Bull," Lamar said. Then McNeil heard the door open and close.

"No need for jail," Doc Holder said.

"Course there is, Doc. What about when he comes around? You think you or a woman can keep him here? He's a dangerous man. And I'm not letting him escape again. It was pure luck we caught him this time."

"I'll keep him sedated. When he comes out from under the chloroform, I'll administer this to him."

With his eyes shut, McNeil saw nothing but assumed Holder was showing Sommers medicine of some kind.

"What is it? Looks like water."

"You should sample it, and you would soon see it's not water. It's opium powder mixed with alcohol, a powerful sedative, good for what ails you. A dose of this every two hours will keep McNeil under for as long as you want."

"All right, fine. With Chick down for a while, that will free Patrick and Grover up to help with the work at the Lazy E. That herd will be here in another two or three days."

"Well, there you go," Patrick said. "Doc can keep him under with that concoction for a few days, so there is no need for a killing. Then, once the herd leaves town with the cows, we're home and dry and can turn him loose."

"Patrick, your brain is about the size of that of a housefly. So don't tax it. Do you forget he's been out to the Lazy E and seen the cattle? He knows too much now and probably has figured out the entire thing."

"Not to mention he has nearly killed me twice," Rhodes said. "My jaw still doesn't feel right, and I want some payback."

"All right, Grover," Sommers said. "When the time is right, you can handle the job."

"Just like Everhart," Rhodes said.

"Shut up about Everhart," Patrick said. "I wasn't a part of that, and I want to know nothing about it."

"Patrick, I think you've turned yellow," Sommers said.

"Hold on, Sommers, I'm not taking that kind of talk from you or anyone else."

"Put that gun away, Patrick!" Sommers exclaimed. "Have you taken leave of your senses? I'm not even armed."

"Then you should've armed yourself before deciding to call me a coward."

"Okay, I apologize. I misspoke."

McNeil heard the door open and close once again before anyone could say more.

"Jay said you needed me, Doc?"

"Yes, Kate. Thanks for coming. I need someone to stay with this man and administer medication to him every two hours. I can't stay with him full time and neglect my other rounds."

"All right, Doc. Just tell me what you need me to do."

"He should come out from under the chloroform soon that I gave him when I removed a bullet fragment from his head wound. When he does, I'll give him a dose of this sedative. Then, I need you to give him one tablespoon full every two hours afterward."

"Sounds simple enough."

"It is important you dose him every two hours without fail, Kate. Giving it to him even a quarter-hour earlier could cause an overdose. That could stop the heart. A quarter-hour too late, and he will awaken. I don't want that either. He needs rest to heal from his wound. The sedative will quiet his mind."

"Got it. I'll give it to him every two hours on the dot."

Holder shook McNeil's shoulder. "Mr. McNeil? Are you awake?"

Figuring he couldn't play possum forever, McNeil opened his eyes."

"How are you feeling, Mr. McNeil?"

"Groggy. My head hurts."

"That's expected. You suffered a bullet wound to the head, and I administered anesthesia before doing surgery."

"Never heard of anyone surviving a bullet wound to the head," McNeil said, pretending to be drowsier than he was.

"You were fortunate," Holder said. "It appears you caught only a bullet fragment from a ricochet. It failed to penetrate your skull, so while painful, you will make a full recovery."

"Good thing I have a hard head."

McNeil felt a hand behind his neck.

"Lift your head, Mr. McNeil. I have some medicine for you."

McNeil lifted his head and opened his mouth. Holder put a spoon to his lips and tipped some bitter-tasting liquid into his mouth."

"Good," Holder said. "The medicine will keep you quiet and still, which will aid your speedy recovery."

Soon after taking the sedative, McNeil felt very sleepy and disoriented. Then he drifted off into an uneasy slumber.

Chapter 12

A New Prescription

THE REST OF THE day and early evening were a blur for McNeil. Under the influence of the sedative, he experienced troubling dreams and hallucinations. He had only vague recollections of Kate giving him more of the bitter-tasting medicine repetitively. At least he thought he recalled it. The effects of the powerful drug compound made it difficult for McNeil to distinguish reality from fanciful imagined images.

Moreover, the sedative didn't always render him fully unconscious. He experienced bouts of wakefulness but always felt woozy, disoriented, and weak. His limbs felt so heavy he didn't have the strength or will to move them. Some thought, deep in the recesses of his mind, plagued him. He was supposed to do something, something of vital importance. But he could never quite grasp what it was he must do.

Perhaps because his body was developing a tolerance to the drug, at times during the night,

McNeil began experiencing slightly more clarity during his brief periods of wakefulness. That's when he finally understood what his mind tried to tell him. He must stop taking the medicine Kate was giving him. But how? Feeling weak as a newborn calf, he didn't have the strength to overpower even a slight girl like Kate.

McNeil didn't know what time of the night he formulated the plan and carried it out. Time had long since ceased to hold any relevance for him. But he knew it was late in the night or early morning because the last time Kate had come in to give him the medicine, she had worn a long cotton nightshirt and looked as though she had just awakened. That time, he had immediately gone back to sleep. But he was awake now.

Summoning all his willpower, McNeil looked at the table beside the bed. He saw the medicine bottle of light blue glass and a glass filled with water that Kate had helped him drink from when he had asked for water. With great effort, McNeil rolled from his back onto his side, facing the table. He willed himself to stretch out his hand for the medicine bottle. It seemed like hours before he managed to accomplish such a simple task, but finally, the bottle was in his grasp. Using his teeth, he removed the cork stopper. Then McNeil tipped the bottle and emptied the contents onto the floor beside the bed. That task accomplished, McNeil felt so sleepy and tired. But he had more to do.

First, after several attempts, McNeil grasped the water glass. Then, leaning over the edge of the bed, he emptied the water into the blue bottle. He spilled some, but got most of it into the bottle. Next, after laying the empty glass on the bed beside him, McNeil replaced the cork in the medicine bottle. His efforts had sapped all his strength, and McNeil soon drifted off to sleep.

A while later, McNeil awakened with a start. He may have slept only minutes or an hour or more, but had no way of knowing. The uncertainty produced a renewed sense of urgency to finish the task, as he feared Kate might return at any minute. It seemed to require superhuman effort, but McNeil managed to replace the medicine bottle on the table. Only one step remained. Taking hold of the empty water glass, McNeil summoned the dregs of his remaining strength and hurled the glass to the floor beside the bed. The effort rewarded him with the satisfying sound of shattered glass. Finally, with the task behind him, McNeil could surrender to the blessed sleep he craved.

It seemed only an instant after he had fallen asleep that McNeil felt a hand on his shoulder shaking him roughly. With great effort, he opened his eyes.

"What happened?" Kate said, with concern etched on her face.

"Sorry," McNeil said with feigned sleepiness. "Thirsty. Tried to reach the water. I must have knocked it off the table. Sorry, Kate."

"That's all right," Kate said soothingly. "I'll clean up the mess and get you another glass of water." Then she left the room.

Moments later, she returned with a broom and towels. She swept up the broken glass and then sopped up the spilled liquid, which she assumed was only water from the broken glass. After finishing, she pushed a lock of hair behind her ear and looked at the clock on the wall.

"Perfect timing," she said. "You need your medicine."

Opening the blue bottle, Kate filled the tablespoon with liquid. Then she helped McNeil raise his head and poured the liquid into his open mouth, unaware that this time it was only water. Finally, she put the cork back in and replaced the bottle on the bedside table. Then she yawned.

McNeil saw she still wore the night clothes and assumed it wasn't morning yet.

"You want water?"

"Yes, please."

Again, the woman helped McNeil raise his head as she put the glass to his lips and helped him drink.

"Thanks."

Kate nodded. "It's almost time for me to get up. If you feel like eating something, I'll feed you breakfast when I return to give you your medicine."

"Thank you. But I'm so sleepy now."

"That's normal. It shows the medicine is working."

⁂

When McNeil next woke, his mind felt clearer, and he felt less tired. He wasn't feeling normal, but better than he had since getting shot. He could tell the effects of the medicine had waned after he'd avoided the last dose. The man hoped that he'd be capable of standing and resisting his captors if necessary in a few more hours. He no longer felt groggy or sleepy. He knew he must fake that until he regained more strength so Kate wouldn't figure out what he had done.

McNeil had recovered his strength by midday, and the drugs were out of his system. Finally, he was ready to act. He waited until Kate came in to administer the medicine. She looked at him, yawned, and put a hand over her mouth.

"Sorry, I'm so sleepy. A woman living about ten miles out of town is having a difficult delivery. Doc has been out there since yesterday. Getting up every two hours all night long has worn me out. I hope he gets back soon. I need about four hours of uninterrupted sleep."

McNeil pretended to be half-asleep as the woman chattered away. She removed the cork from the medicine bottle, filled the spoon, and stepped over to the bed. When Kate reached down to support his head and moved the spoon towards his lips, McNeil grabbed her right wrist causing the spoon to fly from her hand. Then he sprang up, wrestled her down onto the bed, and pinned her body with his as he clapped a hand over her mouth.

"Promise not to scream and behave, and I'll let you up," he said.

Kate looked up at him with wide, fear-stricken eyes.

"I'd not like to hurt you, Kate. But there are people in this town who plan to kill me. You might be one of them. So remember, I'm a desperate man. Also, remember what we talked about before. How desperate people are liable to do things they never imagined ever doing when they are facing a serious threat. Do you promise?"

Kate nodded her head.

Slowly, McNeil removed his hand and got off her. He stood up, and Kate raised herself on her elbows, confused.

Picking up the blue bottle, McNeil held it up. "This is water, pure water. I know because I filled the prescription myself. Thanks for your loving care, but I got a gut full of being drugged."

"I only did what Doc said," Kate whined. "I tried to help you."

"Maybe you believed that," McNeil said. "But you were helping to keep me incapacitated until Sommers got around to killing me."

McNeil seized Kate by the arms and jerked her to her feet, shaking her. "Who killed Denton Everhart and why, Kate?"

"I swear he got sick and died. That's the truth."

"There's more to it than that. You and Sommers both lied about when he died. I saw his grave, and it's not more than a week old. So what is this town covering up?"

"Denton was stubborn. He wouldn't listen to reason."

"I figured it was something like that," McNeil said, shoving the woman violently back onto the bed. Suddenly, he felt repulsed just looking at her.

"I know all about this town's dirty little secret. I know anthrax when I see it, and I know what it looks like when it burns through a herd of cattle. That's what killed those cows I saw out at the Lazy E. That's why Sommers' hands are dragging them into an arroyo and burning the carcasses with kerosene."

"You don't understand! This town needs that cattle money. We won't survive until next year without it. Denton tried to wire those cattlemen to tell them about the anthrax. When he found out Beeson never sent the wire, he was determined to ride to them with a warning. That's why he's dead and why they want you dead."

"Listen, Kate. You want to know what this town's problem is? You want to know what your problem is?"

"I suppose you intend telling me," she retorted.

"I surely do. You people have become so accustomed to living from year to year that you can't see what is as plain as the nose on your pretty face."

"What?"

"Anthrax doesn't make an entire herd of beeves sick at once. Instead, it cuts its way through a herd. It keeps cutting until it burns itself out. So there's bound to be infected cows still out there. Not enough time has passed. And if you mix them with other cows, the infection will spread. What do you think will happen if the ranchers here sell their infected beeves to that herd coming through?"

"I don't care. We'll have the money, money we must have to survive."

"You aren't seeing the big picture, Kate. A few days or a week after they leave here, those drovers will start seeing their cows drop on the trail and die. And from there it will only get worse. The word will spread with the disease. People on the trail will block the trail and refuse to let the herd pass through their territories. The trail boss will have to stop and make camp. Then the cows that anthrax doesn't kill will starve when the grass plays out. Or, if they must stop the drive where there is no water, the cattle will die of thirst."

"That's not our problem."

"Oh, but it is. Think about this. That herd won't make it to Denver. So the trail boss won't get any profits, and his drovers won't get their pay. You think they won't come back to this town with revenge on their minds and murder in their hearts? They may shoot up this town and kill the lot of you. At the very least, they will burn this town to the ground."

"I don't believe you."

"That's because you're naïve. I've been on many of those drives. So I know how those men think. But say they show this town mercy, mercy it doesn't deserve. What about next year? You think anyone is going to stop here to buy cattle again? They won't come within a thousand miles of this place. At best, all you people will do is save yourselves for twelve short months. Then this town will die anyway."

"What are you going to do?"

"Nothing at present. We're going to wait for Doc to return. I need to talk some sense into at least some people in this town before it's too late. If no one listens, then I'll do something else. In the meantime, you and I will stick together like we are joined at the hip. So come one, let's see if the good doctor keeps any firearms on the place."

Chapter 13

Changing Perspectives

BUD LONG STOOD IN his office, his shoulders hunched, staring out the grime-covered window at the dusty street. Doc Holder walked in, but Long didn't turn. Instead, he kept staring out the window without acknowledging his visitor. Holder shifted uncomfortably and watched Long, but didn't speak. The men had been friends for many long years, and Holder knew something was bothering Bud. Finally, Long turned and looked at Holder.

"You look beat, Doc."

"I am beat. I've been out at the Pearson's place for nearly forty straight hours."

"How did it turn out?"

"Not well. The child was stillborn. Nothing I could do."

"That's rough. I'm sorry to hear about it."

"Yes, but they're still young. They can try again."

Long nodded and then walked to his desk and dropped into the chair.

"I've had it, Doc. I truly have."

"What do you mean?"

"Sommers can find himself another boy. I can't take another day of it."

After a long pause, Long continued. "If you're going to be a lawman, people have to respect you. Otherwise, you can't do your job." Long shook his head. "Everyone in town just laughs behind my back. I'm surprised they don't laugh right in my face."

"I don't laugh, Bud."

"Why not?"

"Cut it out, Bud."

"You should. I deserve it."

"Snap out of it, Bud. You're only going through a rough patch."

"A week ago, if I'd done my job—if I'd looked into things and found out what happened—then maybe people would respect me. Maybe I could respect myself. But I didn't. Just like Sommers expected."

"What could you have found out, Bud? They gave you a story, and you had to accept it."

"Do you believe the story?"

Holder squirmed uncomfortably but didn't answer.

"Do you know what happened?"

"I don't know, nor do I want to know. I admit it—I'm not what you would call a brave man. But, heck, I'm probably fooling myself by even saying that. I'm probably a brass-plated coward."

"You're not the only one," Long said. "I didn't even try to find out. Don't you understand, Doc?" Long tapped the star pinned on his chest with two fingers. "When you wear a badge, you're the law. And when someone breaks the law, you're supposed to do something about it. It's your job. Me, I did nothing except climb into a whiskey bottle. That there is what a true coward does, Doc."

There was another long, awkward period of silence.

"I did nothin', Doc. And that's eatin' me alive inside. You got a remedy for that?"

Holder shook his head sadly. "If I did, I'd have prescribed it for myself long ago."

Long unpinned the star and tossed it on the desk. "Sommers can find another boy. I've had it with being a hypocrite. Besides, this job is crowdin' my drinking time."

"You can't quit."

"Why not?"

"That feller lying over there in my surgery, McNeil. Maybe he has a remedy. That's what I stopped in to discuss with you. I suggested sedating him to keep him out of Sommers' clutches, but any day he will show up at my surgery to claim him. Then McNeil will suffer the same fate as Denton Everhart."

"I thought you said you didn't know what happened to Everhart."

"I don't know! Just because I'm a coward doesn't mean I can't speculate as well as anyone else. And I speculate Denton Everhart died of an acute case of lead poisoning."

Long nodded somberly. "That's my thinking too."

The two men looked at each other for several long moments. Then, Long picked up the star and pinned it back on his shirt.

"Maybe we should head over to your place and sober that McNeil feller up. Maybe he can help us find a way out of this mess before that herd shows up and Sommers palms his sick cows off on those unsuspecting boys."

In Doc Holder's desk drawer, McNeil found an 1847 Walker Colt. Originally, the handgun was a .44 caliber percussion revolver designed to hold six charges of black powder and six lead ball bullets. But some gunsmith had converted Holder's pistol to a six-shot .45 caliber Colt cartridge revolver. A Walker Colt would never be a weapon of choice for McNeil because of the pistol's many infamous failings.

First, the pistol was large and heavy. Also, because of the primitive metallurgy of the period, ruptured cylinders after firing were a common occurrence. McNeil had heard many accounts of Walker Colts exploding in the hands of those shooting them with disastrous results. Finally, an inadequate loading lever catch often allowed the loading lever to drop during recoil, locking the action and preventing fast follow-up shots.

Converting the percussion model to cartridges eliminated the most glaring flaws, like the occurrence of ruptured cylinders. But the Walker Colt remained cumbersome. Still, McNeil found it far superior to no weapon and was pleased to find the Walker Colt and a box of cartridges. After checking the action and loading the pistol, he stuck it in the belt of his pants.

At McNeil's urging, Kate brewed coffee, and they sat together in the surgery awaiting Doc Holders' return in uneasy silence.

Chapter 14

Shifting Alliances

KATE LAMAR STOOD AT the window with the curtain's edge pulled back slightly. "Doc is back, and he's not alone."

McNeil got up and strode to the window. He looked out over Kate's shoulder. Holder and the town marshal, Bud Long, came up the path to Doc's establishment—one building serving as home, office, and surgery.

"The marshal will put you back in jail when he sees you're up and about, Pete."

"I don't think so. I've seen enough of that jail to last me. So I'm not going back."

"You mean to go up against the law?"

"I mean to stay out of that jail. And in my estimation, Bud Long isn't much of a lawman."

"Bud Long is not a bad man. But he's between a rock and a hard place and does the best he can under the circumstances."

"Well, his best isn't good enough. A man wearing a badge is supposed to represent the law. When the law gets broken, he has to do something about it. Long does nothing but look the other way and lets Sommers run roughshod all over this town."

"If you don't like it here, why don't you go back to where you came from?"

"I aim to, but only when I'm ready. Only after I've done what I must. You greet them, but don't warn them, Kate. I'll be right back there in the hallway with this." McNeil pulled the Walker Colt from his belt and stalked to the hallway separating the surgery from the residence.

Doc Holder, followed by Marshal Long, entered the surgery. Holder appraised Kate Lamar standing in the middle of the room with a pinched expression on her face and arms crossed.

"Kate, you look a bit peaked," Holder said. "Are you feeling poorly?"

"I'm fine, Doc."

Holder nodded. "Sorry I was away so long. Things were rough out at the Pearson's place. How's the patient?"

"I'm okay, Doc," McNeil said, stepping into the surgery from the hallway with the Walker Colt in his hand."

Holder and Long stood looking at the man in astonishment.

"I wasn't quite as sedated as I let on."

"It's not my fault," Kate exclaimed. "He poured out the medicine and filled the bottle with water."

"Hold on there, young feller," Long said. "Don't do nothing rash. Doc here was only trying to help you."

"Help me? By doping me so Sommers could lay hands on me whenever he got ready? I can think of plenty of words to describe what Doc has done for me. But help isn't one of them."

"Don't you see?" Doc said. "It was the only way to keep you alive. If I hadn't suggested keeping you sedated, Sommers would have insisted that the marshal put you back in jail. Then you would have been at Sommers' mercy."

McNeil studied the man's words. In some ways, they made sense.

"I suppose there might be some truth to what you've said, Doc," he said. Then, turning to Long, he continued. "With all due respect to the law, I'm not going back to jail, Marshal, and no one is doping me again."

"I'm not here to take you back to jail, McNeil. No need. I've dropped the charges."

That news surprised McNeil.

"What did Sommers say about that?"

"Don't know. I didn't consult him."

"Again, no offense, Marshal, but you're under Bull Sommers' thumb, according to my calculations, like everyone else in this town."

Long nodded. "I was. But not anymore. I know you don't respect me, McNeil, and I don't fault you for it. But I'm finished taking orders from Bull Sommers."

"You best not say that to his face, Bud," Kate said. "Those are dangerous words. He might kill you."

"Kate, there are some things worse than dying, things that eat at a man's insides until he feels death might be the better option."

"So, what are you saying, Marshal?" McNeil said.

"I'm saying I know you intend to stand against Sommers. We ain't much, but Doc and me will stand beside you. I have amends to make to this town for not doing my job, and I want to set things right."

"All right," McNeil said, shoving the pistol back in the belt of his pants. "Kate made coffee. Let's sit down around the table and talk things over."

Kate Lamar brought the pot and cups. After serving Doc and the marshal, she refilled McNeil's cup and her own before joining the men at the table.

"Mr. McNeil, you mind telling me your interest in all this?" Long said. "You're not even from here. So what do you care about Dead Horse Crossing?"

"Marshal, I don't give two cents about this town. My interest is purely personal. Someone in this town killed Denton Everhart, a friend of mine. Denton served with me in seventeen different engagements during the war, from Antietam to the Knoxville campaign. He saved my life at Antietam, and he never shirked a duty. Were it not for him, I'd lie now buried far from Texas in the soil of Maryland. I intend to kill those responsible for the murder of my friend and to stop Sommers from selling infected cows to that drive coming up the trail."

"Son, it sounds like you're looking for more than justice for your friend," Holder said. "It sounds like you're seeking a reckoning. But, unfortunately, those two things aren't the same thing."

"They are to me," McNeil said. "I have a good idea who killed Denton, but perhaps you gents can spell out the names for me."

"I wish we could," Holder said. "But neither of us knows for sure. We've only guessed at it the same as you."

McNeil's eyes roved to Kate Lamar.

"Don't look at me, Pete McNeil. I'm not in Bull Sommers' inner circle. I think everyone at this table knows Sommers was behind it. But I'm sure he didn't pull the trigger himself. Instead, he pays others to do his dirty work."

"Perhaps I can answer the question," a new voice said.

McNeil jumped to his feet, whirling toward the speaker, the Walker Colt appearing in his hand as if by magic.

"Woah there, pardner," Patrick said, holding his hands up. He held a burlap sack in his left hand. "I'm only here to parlay. I come in peace. And I'm bearing gifts." Patrick shook the burlap sack.

McNeil relaxed and lowered the pistol.

"What's in the sack?"

"Something I reckon you would like to get back," Patrick said, lowering his hands and rummaging in the sack. Then he pulled out McNeil's holstered Colt with the gun belt wrapped around the holster. "I liberated this from the marshal's desk drawer when I was pulling guard duty at the jail. I knew Grover had his eye on it."

McNeil stepped over and took the holstered pistol from Patrick. "Much obliged to you. What did you want to talk about, Patrick?"

"What we're planning to do about Sommers."

"What we're planning? You dealing yourself a hand in the game?"

"Yeah, might as well. I pulled stakes and folded my tent out at the Bar Deuce. So I'm footloose and fancy-free, looking for a new outfit. I never embraced the idea of selling sick cows to that drive coming in and don't approve of what happened to Denton Everhart."

"A minute ago, you said you could answer my question."

"That I can. I saw Sommers, Fitz Newsome, and Grover Rhodes light out for the Lazy D the evening Everhart got it. And a few days later, I overheard Grover bragging about killing him. I suspect he told the truth about it. But I know Sommers ordered it done. What I don't know is whether Fitz played a role in it."

"Okay, come sit," McNeil said.

He and Patrick joined the others at the table.

"I'll get another cup," Kate said, excusing herself.

"What was Sommers' beef with Denton, anyway?" McNeil said.

"Well, he wanted to push Everhart out so he could take over the Lazy E range for his cattle," Patrick said. "So that's how it started. Sommers had bought another five hundred head down Bandera way. He needed the grass. But it came to a head when the anthrax showed up."

"How so?"

"Everhart insisted on notifying the cattlemen headed this way. But Sommers wouldn't have it."

"They killed him because he disagreed with Sommers?"

"No, Everhart tried to warn the cattlemen. First, he tried telegraphing. But Beeson wouldn't send the wire."

"I can imagine that," Long said. "Beeson won't send a wire to anyone without asking Sommers first. He's too afraid of the man."

Patrick nodded. "Anyway, when Everhart found out Beeson never sent the wire, he was determined to ride south and tell them boys personally. So they killed him to stop him and shut him up for good."

"I saw all the dead beeves on the Lazy E range. Is that where the anthrax started?"

"No, sir. It started on the Bar Deuce after Sommers brought in the cows from Bandera. Anthrax is unusual in these parts, but common down in South Texas. But Sommers was already crowding Everhart's range, and his cows infected those on the Lazy E."

"I don't peg Sommers as an ignorant man," McNeil said. "He's only one of those wealthy men who thinks his money gives him the right to do as pleases. But he must have the sense to know selling diseased cattle to the owners of that herd will poison the well. He'll never get another herd through here."

"Sure he knows," Patrick agreed. "But he doesn't care. Sommers reckons the anthrax is only a run of bad luck. He wants to get the money from the herd owners to cut his losses. Then he'll pack up and pull his freight out of here and start over somewhere else."

"And leave the town to bear the consequences."

Patrick nodded. "You got it." The young cowboy glanced around. "Hey, where did that girl get off to, anyway?. She was supposed to bring me a cup, and I could use some of that coffee."

The mention of Kate startled McNeil. He hadn't noticed she hadn't returned from the kitchen. So he got up to look for her. When he got to the kitchen, he found the back door standing open, but no sign of Kate Lamar.

After returning from the kitchen, McNeil looked at Patrick. "Did you come in the back door?"

"Yeah, I didn't want anyone seeing me come through the front door."

"Did you shut the door?"

"Yeah, why?"

"It's open now. Seems Kate Lamar was tired of our company and has run off."

"That tears it," Doc Holder said. "She will go straight to her no-account brother Jay and tell him what we've discussed. Then you can bet Jay will go to Sommers and tell him."

"Well, no use cryin' over spoiled milk," Patrick said. "Sommers was bound to find out, anyway. Besides, he's running out of time. That herd will hit town soon." Patrick pointed his finger at McNeil. "So he will make his move to get rid of this feller soon."

Chapter 15

The Gambit

BULL SOMMERS SAT IN a leather-covered stuffed chair behind a large, ornate wooden desk inside his ranch house at the Bar Deuce. Pencil in hand and his head bent to the task, the rancher made notations on the page of a large, thick ledger book. Then, spurs jangling, Grover Rhodes strode into the room.

"Boss, Cotton Patrick ain't at the bunkhouse."

Sommers sighed and laid the pencil on the desk. He leaned back in the chair, pinched the bridge of his prominent nose between thumb and forefinger, and then glared at Rhodes.

"Can't you follow simple instructions, Grover? I distinctly recall telling you to find Patrick and bring him to me. I didn't intend for you to look in one place and then return to tell me Patrick wasn't there. Find him!"

"I mean, he ain't on the ranch, boss. He ain't out working stock. The boys at the bunkhouse say he packed up and cleared out. He's quit."

Sommers' face flushed red. That tendency when he grew angry had given rise to his nickname, Bull. That and his thick neck.

"Nobody quits this outfit without my permission."

"All I know is Patrick hauled his freight out of here."

"Where did he go?"

"No one knows. But, boss, maybe it's for the best. Patrick did his work, but he was a troublemaker. He never cottoned to the idea of selling the beeves to the owners of the herd coming in when anthrax hit us. And he made no secret he reckoned someone killed Everhart. And he didn't like that either."

"That's what concerns me," Sommers said. "What if that darn fool got the notion in his head to do what Everhart aimed to do?"

"I don't think Patrick is that ignorant," Rhodes said.

"Grover, I told you to leave the thinking to me. You're not equipped for it."

Rhodes hunched his shoulders and dropped his head. "Uh, boss, Patrick ain't the only one who pulled stakes and quit."

"What!" Sommers exclaimed, jumping to his feet.

Without making eye contact, Rhodes said, "Appears Patrick ran his mouth off before leaving. He mentioned the McNeil feller and spread it around that there was a fight coming and they would go up against a genuine gunfighter. When Smitty saw them packing up and asked where they were going, they told him they had hired on as cowpunchers, not gun hands."

Sommers paced the room with his hands clasped behind his back. Finally, he stopped and turned to look at Rhodes.

"That Patrick is just dumb enough and reckless enough to ride south to warn off that trail boss to spite me. So, Grover, take two of the boys and three fast horses. Head southeast for about eight hours on the cattle trail toward Young County. If you don't overtake Patrick, after eight hours of riding, find some high ground where you can watch the trail. Then wait there for one of two things to happen."

"What two things?"

"If you see Cotton Patrick on the trail, kill him, and come back. Say nothing to him. Don't ask him questions. Just kill him. Understand?"

Rhodes nodded emphatically.

"If the herd shows up, and you haven't seen Patrick by then, get back here fast. That will mean Patrick didn't carry a warning to them, and we don't need to worry about him."

"But what about McNeil?"

"Don't worry. We'll take care of McNeil soon enough. Right now, Doc Holder has him sedated. He isn't going anywhere. So you will be back in plenty of time to get in on it, no matter what happens on the trail. I told you before. You get the first crack at him."

Rhodes nodded. "There are only eight men left at the bunkhouse. Who do you want me to take along?"

"Are Fitz Newsome and Len Johnson still with us?"

"Yes, I saw them both at the bunkhouse."

"Okay, then I'll leave that up to you, Grover. Take whoever you want, except for Newsome and Johnson. I may need them for something else before you get back. Just make sure the two you take aren't squeamish about killing Patrick."

"Okay, boss. We'll leave within the hour."

"Good, get going."

—⁓—

Cotton Patrick looked at McNeil with disbelief etched on his face.

"Say what?"

"I want you to ride south on the cattle trail towards Young County until you find that herd. Tell the trail boss there is anthrax here, and he should give Dead Horse Crossing a wide berth if he doesn't want to end up with a lot of dead cows."

"I don't think you understood what I said, McNeil. I tried to discourage as many of the Bar Deuce hands as possible before leaving. And a good many of them cleared out when I did. But, Sommers will still come against you with between ten and twenty guns. You're already short-handed as it is. So, I think I ought to stay here for the fight."

"Cotton, it's the only option. We can't get a wire out. Beeson won't send it. I can't go. Doc won't be any use in the fight, but we will need him here after the shooting starts. So that only leaves you and Bud. You're a far better horseman, and I know you're familiar with the trail. And I trust you. Don't you see? You're the only choice for the job. We have to get the word to them."

Patrick scratched his chin. "Okay, McNeil, I'll do it. But I'm not too fond of the idea. I feel like I'm running out on you and the town."

McNeil placed a hand on the young cowboy's shoulder. "No, you're not running out on anybody. You will accomplish the most important part of this. You might even save your town."

Patrick nodded. "Okay, I'll grab some supplies and get riding."

As the desert sun, like a fiery orange ball, sunk toward the Llano Estacado horizon, the lone rider bent low in the saddle over the horse's neck as the big buckskin hammered southeast down the

Goodnight-Loving trail from the Pecos towards Young County.

Chapter 16

Council of War

AFTER COTTON PATRICK LEFT, Bud Long, Doc Holder, and McNeil sat at the table late into the afternoon working on a plan for taking on Bull Sommers and his men. Then, finally, Doc went to the kitchen and got supper working around six o'clock while the marshal and McNeil continued the discussion.

"I agree Doc should stay out of the fight," Long said. "So, with only the two of us, I guess we could fort up in the jail to hold them off. It's the most solid building in town."

McNeil shook his head. "We won't fort up, Marshal. The jail still has a wood roof. They could set fire to it, burn us out, and shoot us down when we ran out. Besides, fighting from any building would limit our ability to maneuver."

Then what do you aim for us to do?"

"If we're to have any chance, we have to meet them head on in the street in front of the hotel."

"We just go at it face to face?"

"Yeah. I'm almost certain they will be overconfident because they will outnumber us by a wide margin. Especially with us standing there right in front of them. But we will use that to our advantage."

"You seem to know a lot about these things, McNeil. So you tell me what to do, and I'll do my best."

"I don't mean to be hard, Marshal, but have you ever been in a fight?"

"Not lately. I mean, I was in a few scrapes as a youngster, but never nothing like this. But I'll stand and fight. I won't run if that's what's worrying you."

"I don't doubt your grit, Marshal. I'm only trying to prepare you for what's ahead of us. Once it starts, it will get messy fast. It will be something like you've never seen, maybe never imagined."

Long nodded woodenly. "Keep talking. I'm listening."

"I don't figure on many of them being killers, given what Cotton told me. Probably only a few have ever done any killing at all. They will mostly be cowpunchers with more experience roping and branding cows than handling a six-gun in a stand-up fight. They won't be eager to line up in front of us. And once it starts, I expect most will scatter for cover."

"How about that Fitz Newsome feller Cotton mentioned? That name mean anything to you?"

"He's a killer. He made a name for himself up in New Mexico Territory in the Lincoln County War. Last I heard, he was still up there. So Newsome must be on the dodge down here because of something bad that happened up there."

"Is he as fast as Cotton says?"

"He's fast. But that's not what a fight like this is about, Marshal. It's not like two men facing each other to see who is the fastest draw."

"Would you know him if you saw him?"

"I'll know him. He won't be hard to pick out of the bunch if you know what to look for, Marshal. And we have to take him out of the fight right at the start. I'll point him out to you when we're walking up. I'll be looking first to Rhodes and Sommers. You can take Newsome out with that messenger scattergun of yours."

"The scattergun?"

"Yes, here's what we'll do. I'll use their overconfidence in their numbers against them. So, I'll start out by jawing at them, making them think we're scared and posturing. Then, I'll give them only a split second to think over my words, and then I'll start shooting. It will give us a split-second advantage. I'll do for Rhodes and Sommers. When I start in, you unload on Newsome with that messenger gun. When you've emptied both barrels, throw it down and pull your pistol."

"But you said they would probably scatter quickly."

"They will. I'll have one of your Winchesters. We'll stash the other and ammunition at the livery across the street from the hotel. So soon as you pull your pistol, make a run for the stable for the other. I'll do the same if I can. Then it's going to be root or die, working the sides of the street doing for the others who choose to stand and fight. If we're lucky, some of those cowhands will cut and run when the lead starts flying. Just remember to keep moving forward, Marshal. If you freeze up and stand still, they will cut you down."

"Sounds like you have it all planned out."

"Yeah, except for the part about you and me not getting killed."

"I'm thinking about getting out of the marshal business when this is over."

"You will do fine, Marshal. And if you survive this, you should survive most anything else you ever face afterward."

⁓ℓℓ⁓

After supper, Doc Holder encouraged McNeil to stay at his place.

"You don't have to sleep in the surgery," he said. "I have a spare room you can use."

"Much obliged, Doc, but I'm moving back into the hotel. And I want to find out about Kate Lamar if I can."

"Well, since I'm not part of the war council, I'm turning in for the night," Holder said. "I hardly got any sleep the last forty-eight hours, and I'm too old for that."

"Okay, night, Doc."

Holder bid his friend Long goodnight and left for bed.

"When do you think they will come for us?" Long said.

"Don't know, but with that herd getting close, I don't expect they will wait much longer. Sommers may try to probe us first, before the big fight commences, especially if he knows I'm no longer incapacitated. He'll want to find out what he's up against first."

"Maybe if the herd is close, Cotton will get there and back before the shooting starts. Then it would be three of us at least."

"That would be good if it played out that way, but we can't count on it. It depends on where that drive is right now. Kate said the trail boss wires the town when they are a day or two away. But I don't expect Sommers will share the word with us."

"I expect you're right. Once Sommers finds out I've quit him, he won't tell me anything."

McNeil and Bud Long left Doc Holder's place and went their separate ways—Long to his house in town and McNeil to the hotel. McNeil's expectations for the marshal weren't too high. He believed the man had good intentions, but you never knew what a man with little experience with something like they would soon face would do when the shooting started. McNeil only hoped Bud Long could account for Newsome and maybe one other with his coach gun when the fight started. He knew his chances of survival would improve measurably if that happened. But if Sommers mustered twenty guns to come at them with, the higher end of Cotton's prediction, it wouldn't matter much, anyway. He and Long would both get killed.

Chapter 17

A Missing Woman

Jay Lamar hadn't been present when McNeil had returned to the hotel the previous evening. Finding his room as he had left it, his belongings undisturbed, heartened him. But when he walked downstairs after waking in search of breakfast, Lamar was at the front desk. The man eyed him coldly.

"I thought you were at Doc Holder's place under care," Lamar said.

"My condition is much improved, so I'm back here now," McNeil said.

"Then where's my sister? I'd assumed she was still helping the doc care for you."

"She left Holder's place early yesterday afternoon," McNeil said. "I'm going to her place down the street now to see her and have breakfast."

"Kate is not there. Her hired man is still running the place. Nor was she at home when I left this morning."

The news troubled McNeil. "Where do you think she's gone?"

"I don't have the foggiest notion," Lamar said.

"Maybe she is back home by now," McNeil said. "Tell me where you live, and I'll go there now to check."

"No, by thunder. She's not your lookout. Kate is my sister. I'll check on her myself. I'm worried now that you've told me she left Doc Holder's yesterday afternoon." Lamar came round the desk on his way to the door.

McNeil followed. "I'm going with you, welcome or not."

Lamar snorted, but then eyed the tied-down Colt on the man's hip. "Suit yourself."

The men left the hotel for Lamar's place. They passed quickly up the boardwalk to Kate's eating establishment. Jay Lamar ducked inside to see if Kate had turned up there. He exited a moment later.

"They still haven't seen her," he said to McNeil.

The men continued walking in silence and turned onto a secondary street. After a short distance, they came to a house of undistinguished architecture and went inside.

"Kate!" Jay Lamar shouted, but to no avail. He received no answer. The men searched the house but found no sign of Kate.

Returning to the sitting room, Jay exclaimed, "Pa's Henry rifle isn't above the mantel! That's where we keep it."

"You think your sister took it?"

"Sometimes Kate gets a hankering for wild game and goes hunting."

"Alone?"

"Sure. My sister rides and shoots a rifle as well as any man."

"She owns a horse, then?"

"Yes, she keeps a horse down at the livery."

"Let's go," McNeil said.

The men retraced their steps and went into the livery across the street from the hotel. The grizzled old liveryman, Sam, paused his work, leaning on the handle of a pitchfork, and looked at them inquiringly.

"Have you seen my sister, Sam?"

"Yeah, yesterday afternoon when she came in for her horse."

"Did Kate say where she was headed?" McNeil asked.

"No, she didn't. But she was totin' a rifle. So I supposed she was going huntin' again."

"Maybe her horse took a fall or went lame," Jay said with worry etched on his face.

"Where does she generally go hunting?"

"Well, lately, out to the Lazy E ranch. Kate was sweet on Everhart. Though I didn't approve of it, I expected they would marry soon."

"Maybe you should catch your horse and ride out to the Lazy E spread and look for her," McNeil said. "I'm not at liberty to leave town at the moment to go with you. I may have important business to attend to here at any time."

"What's happening?" Jay said.

"That's not your concern, Lamar. Just worry about finding your sister." With that, McNeil turned on his heel and walked across the street to the hotel.

About an hour after McNeil watched from his seat on the boardwalk in front of the hotel, Jay Lamar spurring a sorrel pony north on his way out of town,

Bud Long sat down in the chair beside him. Long had two Winchesters and his messenger gun with him, along with an armload of ammunition.

"Thought I'd bring the guns and ammunition over from the jail," Long said. "Never know when we'll need them, I guess."

"Good thinking, Marshal," McNeil said. "I'll take one rifle and some ammunition over the livery in a spell and stash it there for our later use."

The marshal nodded. "I had an inspiration," he said. "I talked to the menfolk around town, trying to drum up some recruits. But no one wants to tangle with Sommers."

"It's just as well, Marshal. Stable hands and shopkeepers would only get killed in the fight we face. It's our responsibility. I'm in it by choice, and you by duty. We can't look to the townsfolk."

"I don't want you to think too poorly of the people in this town," Long said. "There are some solid citizens here. They are just fearful of Sommers. But, I'll tell you, this town was on its last legs when Sommers first rode in here. He flashed his money about and gave folks hope the town might endure. Then, using his wealth, Sommers tightened the noose around all our necks and took over little by little. We didn't realize we'd struck a bargain with the devil until it was too late."

"It's a well-known story in the west," McNeil said. "Arrogant men with much often take advantage of those with less or nothing."

Long nodded. "Did you get the chance to talk to Kate Lamar?"

"No, I neglected to mention it, but Kate has gone missing. Her brother is out looking for her now."

"Gone missing?"

"Yes, after she ran away from Doc Holder's yesterday, she didn't return home, and no one has seen her. Except for Sam at the livery. She called there yesterday afternoon for her horse."

"Where does Jay think she's gone?"

"He speculated she may have gone hunting. But if so, it seems she should be back by now."

"What if Sommers has her?"

"Sommers? Why would he take Kate Lamar?"

"Well, maybe Kate rode out to the Bar Deuce to tell him what she overheard at Doc's place. Kate loves this town and, from the start, supported Sommers' intention to get the cattle sold and anthrax be hanged. She might have gone to warn him of our intentions, though I suspected she'd only reveal what she knew to her brother and leave it to him to tell Sommers."

"But you still haven't explained why Sommers would have kept her at his ranch if she rode out there."

"I'm comin' to that. That cur dog, Grover Rhodes, spread it around town that he caught you sparkin' Kate the day of the run-in at her eatin' place. He said Kate was all for it. If Sommers believed the story, he might be holding her hostage—to use as leverage against you. If he thinks Kate has a special meaning to you, he might believe having her as a hostage will affect your calculations."

"Even the vilest men in the west rarely molest innocent women."

"Well, Sommers doesn't have to harm Kate. He only needs to convince you he's willing for the plan to work."

"Well, I'd not like seeing the woman come to any harm, but Kate Lamar means nothing to me. Grover Rhodes spread a lie. Besides, there is nothing we can do, Marshall. We'd need a dozen men at least to storm the Bar Deuce. If he has Kate and you and I went out there alone, we'd probably only get her hurt or killed."

"So, we're just going to wait around and see how it plays out?"

"As I see it, that's all we can do."

"I suppose you're right, McNeil. But even though Kate was on the wrong side of things with supporting selling those diseased cattle, I'd sure hate seeing her in a jackpot. She's a good woman. This town ain't much, but it's Kate's home, and she doesn't want to see it die."

"We can't worry about Kate Lamar at present," McNeil said. "She made her choice when she left us." The bitterness of his declaration convinced Long the man would brook no argument in the matter.

Chapter 18

A Plan Foiled

RHODES, RED SMITH, AND Billy Riley lay in the dirt atop a scrub-covered knob next to the cattle trail. Rhodes peered northwest through the brass spyglass from his saddlebag. The men had ridden hard for almost eight hours without overtaking Cotton Patrick. Then, following Sommers' orders, they had encamped on the knob to watch the trail. It wasn't much of a hill as far as hills go. But it was the highest point in the vicinity, with a good view of the flat lands below. The men also hadn't seen hide nor hair of any approaching herd from the southwest, not even a dust cloud.

"I'd rather be sittin' in that cool saloon back in Dead Horse Crossing playin' cards and drinkin' rye than lying about amongst these prickly pears," Smith grumbled. "It's hot as old Hades out here."

"Smitty, you'd always rather be playin' cards and drinkin' whiskey when there's work to do," Riley laughed.

"But long as you're acceptin' your forty and found from Bull Sommers, you'll do what he says," Rhodes said. Then he went back to looking through the glass.

"Cotton has more sense than to go up against the boss," Smith retorted. "We're just wastin' time."

"Hey," Rhodes exclaimed. "Someone is comin' down the trail."

"Is it him?" Riley said, levering a cartridge into the breech of his rifle. "Is it Cotton, sure enough?"

"It's him," Rhodes confirmed. "I'd know that horse anywhere. I've had a hankering to own that gelding for a long while. Pretty soon, I will."

Rhodes collapsed and put down the spyglass as the horse and rider drew closer. Then he snatched the Winchester from Riley's hands.

"Hey, what in Sam Hill you doin'?" Riley complained.

"We can't be foolin' about with this," Rhodes said, sighting down the barrel. "I'm taking the shot myself, Riley. You never could hit anything with this rifle."

Rhodes waited until he was confident of the range, then he took a deep breath. Then, after letting out half of it, he slowly squeezed the trigger until the gun discharged. An instant later, with the crack of the gunshot still echoing around the empty landscape, the rider toppled from the saddle. The horse continued galloping southwest, but the rider lay still, face down on the trail.

"She's done," Rhodes said with satisfaction as he got off the ground. Smith and Riley got to their feet and stared down at the body.

"Now I'll catch that gelding, and we'll take a fast ride back to Dead Horse Crossing," Rhodes said.

"I want his Colt," Smith declared.

"Old Cotton might have some money in his pockets, too," Riley said.

"Yeah, and he won't need it where he's gone," Smith chuckled.

"Okay, ride down and make sure he's dead," Rhodes said. "Once I catch the horse, we're pullin' out."

The men saddled their broncs and rode down the hill. Smith and Riley made for the body while Rhodes went the other way after the rider's horse.

—ece—

Cotton Patrick lay face down in the dirt, stunned. But slowly, as his faculties returned, he realized someone had shot him, and he was sure they had hit him badly. He reckoned the shot had come from the knob, a way to the right of the trail. But, not expecting an ambush, he had paid it no mind. Struggling for breath and spitting blood, the cowboy crawled around until he faced the hill. Then, with difficulty, he drew his Colt. He figured the coyote who shot him would come to make sure he was dead and maybe check him for property to steal. Then he lay his head back on the ground to wait, playing dead. Not that it took much effort. The bullet took him in the left shoulder, but he was bleeding like a stuck hog. The cowboy knew if the shock didn't get him first, he'd soon bleed out.

—ece—

At the base of the hill, Smith and Riley turned their ponies toward the downed rider while Rhodes spurred his horse south to catch Patrick's horse. When Smith and Riley reached the body, they dismounted.

"Yeah, that's old Cotton," Riley said. "I hate seein' this. He wasn't a bad feller."

"The Colt is mine," Smith said. "And if he's got money, we're splittin' it."

Riley turned on him to argue. Patrick recognized the voices. He raised his head and the Colt and shot them both. Then, after they fell, he shot both men in the head to make sure they were dead.

"You boys did for me, and now I've done for you," Patrick said. Then the pistol fell from his hand, and he collapsed.

When Rhodes galloped up a few minutes later, he shot from the saddle, putting two more slugs into Patrick's back. But Patrick was long past feeling it. He had already drawn his last breath. Rhodes looked at the scene in disbelief. Somehow, Patrick had killed Smitty and Riley. Then, catching up the reins of Patrick's gelding again, Rhodes wheeled and lit out northeast up the trail. Having no shovel nor the inclination to bury the dead, Rhodes left it up to the coyotes and vultures to do for the three dead men.

McNeil sat alone cleaning his pistol and Holder's Walker Colt in his hotel room. He had tried to give the gun back to Holder, but Doc told him to keep it since he'd probably have more need of it. McNeil wasn't partial to the old dragoon pistol, but given the odds he would face, it couldn't hurt to have a second pistol stuck in the back of his gun belt. Marshal Long had left on his rounds but had told McNeil he'd call on him again later. So, with heightened senses, McNeil eagerly awaited the coming fight. He wanted to get it over and done. As a rule, he didn't hunt trouble by starting fights. But he always ended them when trouble found him.

Chapter 19

A Prelude

Long about sundown, Rhodes rode up in front of the Bar Deuce ranch house. Wearily, he climbed down and tied both horses to the hitching rail. Then he went into the house to find Sommers and Jay Lamar in the sitting room. Lamar, who had been talking when Rhodes strode through the door, stopped mid-sentence. Both men stood and turned to look at Rhodes.

"Well?" Sommers said.

"We caught Patrick coming down the trail."

"Dead?"

"Yeah, but somehow he got the drop on Smitty and Riley when they rode to him to make sure of it. He killed them both. I had to finish him with my pistol."

"What! You incompetent louts! You should have downed him with a rifle from a distance."

"We did, but I guess the bullet didn't kill him right off."

"Obviously. A dead man couldn't have killed Smitty and Riley. And now I'm down two more men."

"Sorry, boss. That's just how things turned out. It was a bad break. Now, with your permission, I'm heading to the bunkhouse. I'm dead on my feet."

"Go ahead. I'm about to ride into town with Jay."

"Why?"

"Jay says that McNeil is up and about, and I want to know why. Also, Kate Lamar is missing. I have a feeling McNeil is hiding her somewhere."

"Well, then I guess I better go with you."

"No, get some shut-eye. I'll take Fitz and Len Johnson with me."

"But, boss, you promised I'd get first chance at nailin' McNeil's hide to the fence."

"We will not kill McNeil yet. I'm only after information on this trip. Someone else in town brought word that Bud Long and McNeil have become thick as thieves. I want to see what the devil has got into Bud."

"Okay, boss. Then I'll go catch me a nap."

* * *

Bud Long and McNeil sat in the hotel lobby talking.

"Heard anything from Jay about Kate?" Long said.

"Nope. I haven't even seen him since he rode out of town this morning."

"Where could that girl have got off to, anyway?"

"Well, it's looking like you were right when you speculated Sommers might be holding her out at the Bar Deuce."

"If he is, I guess we'll get word soon enough. I mean, if he intends on using her as leverage."

"Guess so," McNeil said.

The men heard horses galloping up out front. They remained seated. Sommers and Jay Lamar walked in when the door opened, followed by two cowhands.

"Where's my sister?" Lamar said to McNeil.

"Why ask me? If you've been out at the Bar Deuce, I'm surprised you didn't find her."

Lamar seemed confused.

"Kate hasn't been out to the ranch," Sommers said. "As I expect you well know."

"Well, I haven't seen her since yesterday afternoon," McNeil said.

Sommers turned his steely gaze on Bud Long. "Marshal, why isn't this man in jail?"

"I dropped the charges."

"What? Care to explain that?"

"Old Sam says he can't recall whether he locked the livery. So, we can't be sure any break-in occurred. And since nothing was missing but McNeil's horse and saddle, it appears there was no crime."

"Well, what about jail breaking and assaulting my hand?"

"Since I arrested McNeil by mistake, I don't see how any of that amounts to a crime."

McNeil studied one cowhand while Sommers argued with the marshal. The powerfully built man with wide shoulders and a narrow waist leaned against the wall with a wolfish grin. But what caught McNeil's educated eye were the two tied-down Colts belted around his waist. McNeil figured one gun was enough for a man who knew how to use it. But he'd known many gunfighters who preferred two. The man was no ordinary cowpuncher. McNeil knew this man was Fritz Newsome, a killer. He wished for the gun belt and Colt he'd left upstairs in his room when the marshal arrived. Unfortunately, the marshal wasn't wearing a gun either.

Sommers had advanced to stand before Bud Long as the argument grew more heated. Suddenly, Sommers stretched forth a hand and ripped the tin star from Long's chest, tearing the man's broadcloth shirt.

"Hey, you can't do that," McNeil exclaimed, the action kindling his sudden rage.

"I think I just did," Sommers said. "The town marshal in Dead Horse Crossing serves at my pleasure. It's no longer my pleasure having Bud Long as marshal. He's incompetent and ineffective."

Bud Long stood with hunched shoulders, looking at the floor. Sommers turned and tossed the badge to Newsome.

"Pin that on, Fritz. You're the town marshal now."

Newsome grinned and pinned the star on his chest.

"And as your first official act, Marshal, arrest that man," Sommers said, pointing his finger at McNeil."

"I don't think I'll let you arrest me this evening, Newsome," McNeil said, adopting a fighting stance.

The badge-wearing gunman grinned and palmed his twin Colts in the blink of an eye.

"McNeil is unarmed," Bud Long exclaimed. "You kill him, and it's cold-blooded murder." Then, wheeling to face Sommers, Long said, "This isn't like the murder of Denton Everhart, Sommers. This time there are witnesses who won't keep quiet. I'll find a way to get word to a federal marshal. Your man will hang, and you will too, as an accessory."

Sommers looked from Long to Jay Lamar.

"I won't say anything, Bull, you know that," Lamar said. "That fool Bud is talking for himself, not me."

"Sure, that's what he says now," Long said. "But he will always have something on you, Sommers, and the day will come when he needs it. Then he'll tell it alright. So, if you're going to murder McNeil, you better kill Jay and me while you're at it."

Sommers looked less sure of himself.

"It's your call," Newsome hissed to Sommers. "Appears to me he's resisting arrest."

"Put your guns away," Sommers said finally.

"But—"

"I said put them away," Sommers thundered. "We won't shoot an unarmed man. But there is more than one way to skin a cat."

"Understanding Sommers' meaning, Len Johnson smiled and stepped forward. He, too, was a big, muscular man, but modestly shorter than Newsome.

"I'll handle the light work, boss," Johnson said to Sommers, unbuckling his gun belt and handing it to Newsome to hold.

"That's right, Len," Sommers said with an ugly grin. "I'm appointing you as a deputy marshal. Now take that man into custody."

Johnson stepped forward confidently, like a man accustomed to having his way with his fists. But McNeil was ready. Like an uncoiling spring, his arm shot forward like a battering ram. His clenched fist struck Johnson squarely in the face. The straight right punch sent Johnson reeling backward, his feet moving ever faster and his arms windmilling as the man sought to keep from falling. Finally, Johnson's back hit the hotel's front door with such force it knocked the door outward off its hinges, and Johnson landed on his back on the boardwalk outside. The man sat up, shaking his head like an angry bull. Then, getting to his feet, he strode back into the lobby with an evil grin, wiping the blood from his nose and mouth with the back of his hand.

Sommers put a concerned hand on Johnson's shoulder, but Johnson shook it off as we went by. "Let me have him," he bellowed, advancing and throwing a mighty roundhouse right at McNeil's head.

McNeil slipped the punch with ease. After it sailed harmlessly above his head, he spun around to face Johnson again. The force of Johnson's swing and miss had sent him sprawling onto the front desk. He righted himself, turned around, and pushed off the desk. Warier now, he approached McNeil with both fists up. McNeil held a similar fighting position, and the two men slowly circled each other. McNeil feinted with his left, causing Johnson to snap his head back to avoid the punch. Then McNeil threw a right hook, but Johnson avoided it. The men continued moving in a tight circle. McNeil feinted with his left twice more. Sensing an advantage, after the second feint, Johnson stepped in, throwing a roundhouse left. But, McNeil slipped the punch by ducking, and when he came out of the crouch, he backhanded Johnson across the face with his left fist and followed up with a right jab that rocked Johnson back on his heels and caused him to fall once again against the front desk. Pushing off it, Johnson stalked forward with a look of fierce determination. But the man now felt doubt. Each time McNeil had landed punches, Johnson felt as if he had been mule-kicked. He had never faced a fighting man like this and was no longer confident he could best this man, McNeil.

Finally, Johnson landed a punch, a right cross that caught the left side of McNeil's head. But McNeil shook it off and landed a straight right, left hook, and right cross combination before Johnson had got his fists back up. Johnson landed on his backside on top of a parlor table, knocking the lamp to the floor. In a frenzy, Jay Lamar rushed over to stomp out the flames from the burning kerosene spilled onto the wood floor by the broken lamp.

Johnson sat upon the edge of the table, glaring at McNeil. But he remained seated there for a moment, allowing his head to clear. Then, with less enthusiasm now, he stood and advanced toward McNeil. Continuing to circle, both men threw punches, and the fight began in earnest. Johnson landed punches, but McNeil landed three or four blows in quick succession for each of his. Johnson threw a left hook, and as McNeil ducked to slip the punch, Johnson connected with a straight right. He tried to follow it with another left, but McNeil came out of his crouch with a right uppercut that caught Johnson squarely beneath the chin and dazed him. Johnson swung, hitting McNeil with a left cross. McNeil countered with a left cross of his own, followed immediately with a right cross. Johnson saw two men now instead of only one through eyes that refused to focus, and both of them had blindingly quick fists.

When Johnson fell again against the front desk, McNeil punched him repeatedly with left and right combinations that forced Johnson to reel drunkenly along the length of the desk, clinging to it with his left hand to avoid falling. When the desk ended, Johnson went to a knee, and McNeil hit him with another powerful left and right combination, sending Johnson to his back on the floor. The big man groaned loudly but somehow got back up to a knee. But when he looked up at McNeil standing over him, the man hit him with another strong left hook. Teeth flew from Johnson's mouth as he landed again on his back on the floor, this time unconscious.

McNeil turned away to face Sommers. Sweat poured from his face, and his shirt was soaked with it, but his breathing was normal. "Anyone else care to try his luck?"

Sommers shrunk away from the man. Then, anxiously, Newsome reached for his guns. But he froze when he heard behind him the unmistakable metallic sound of someone levering a cartridge into the breech of a repeating rifle.

"That's enough," a raspy but determined voice exclaimed.

Every man in the room, save the unconscious Johnson, turned to look at Sam, the old liveryman standing in the broken doorway holding a Winchester pointed at Fritz Newsome.

"Reach for those fancy pistols, sonny, and see what happens. From this distance, I'll blow a hole clean through you with this Winchester big enough for us to all look through."

Newsome shook his head and raised his hands to shoulder level.

"Tarnation!" Sam exclaimed. "It's gettin' where a man can't catch a wink of sleep in this darn town, and the noise from this darn hotel is gettin' worse than the saloon."

"Sam, you old fool," Sommers exclaimed. "Lower that rifle now if you know what's good for you. Coming against me is a mighty dangerous proposition."

"Yeah, I'll put her down soon as you and your fancy gunman there back on out here, draggin' the carcass of the one on the floor behind you."

Sam circled the room, keeping the rifle aimed at the chest of Newsome, giving Sommers and his man access to the hotel's ruined front doorway. Tension filled the room as Sommers glared back at Sam. Finally, with a jerk of his head toward the unconscious Johnson, he walked over to the man, followed by Newsome. They got Johnson to his feet between them, each of them draping a lifeless arm over their shoulders. Then, slowly, they walked the man to the doorway with the toes of his boots dragging along the floor.

Stopping in the doorway, Sommers spoke without turning. "This isn't over. Not by a long shot. You've played hob, McNeil. But you won't leave this town alive, and that's a promise."

"Git movin' Sommers," Sam insisted, prodding the man's back with the rifle muzzle. "I'm missin' out on my beauty sleep. That always makes me mighty disagreeable, and this old Winchester might go off."

Sommers and Newsome continued outside with their burden without another word. They put Johnson in the saddle, then mounted their horses. McNeil, Long, and Lamar had followed Sam out onto the boardwalk. McNeil saw a sight that made him feel like he had been gut-punched.

"Where did you get that gelding?" McNeil said to Sommers.

Sommers shot him a self-satisfied grin. "Seems Cotton Patrick met with a tragic end on the cattle trail southwest of here. He no longer needs a horse. This gelding belongs to Grover Rhodes now, and he gave me the loan of it. Patrick was a fool like you, McNeil. Guess he didn't consider me smart enough to be on the lookout for someone riding to take word to those cattlemen? All he did was get himself killed."

Sommers and Newsome turned their horses and rode slowly away, with Johnson and his mount between them.

Chapter 20

Bewildered

JAY LAMAR AND BUD Long worked on the busted front door, trying to make temporary repairs. McNeil sat in a chair with his elbows on his knees and his face in his hands. He thought about the young blond-haired cowboy, Cotton Patrick, and how he had sent the man to his death. McNeil blamed himself for not anticipating that Sommers might have put men on the trail to watch it. If only he had, he would have instructed Patrick to go by a roundabout way, to stay well away from the well-known cattle trail. But it was too late for that. Too late for Cotton Patrick. McNeil made a mistake, and another man paid for it. A kid not yet twenty-five had paid with everything he had, everything he would ever have had. McNeil felt as low as he recalled feeling in a long time.

Long came over and put a comforting hand on McNeil's shoulder.

"You can't blame yourself for what happened to Cotton Patrick," he said. "Sommers ordered it, and Grover Rhodes murdered that boy. They are at fault. And Cotton was a young man, but a grown man, and it was him who decided to throw in with us."

"One thing I don't need is someone telling me how blameless I am," McNeil said. "I should have foreseen Sommers would send men to watch the trail. If for no other reason, he would have wanted to make sure I didn't ride out of town."

"Like I said before, you can't blame yourself."

"Listen, marshal, I know you mean well, but don't you ever tire of hearing yourself talk?"

"The reason I know so well how you feel is that I've fallen into the same trap. I blame myself, too, and not only for Cotton Patrick. If I'd done my job instead of caving in to Sommers demands all that time, this town could have avoided a lot of bad things. Ripping that star off my shirt might have been the kindest thing Sommers ever did for this town."

Doc Holder bustled into the hotel lobby carrying his beat-up leather medical case.

"I just heard," he said breathlessly. "Old Sam came and told me. He said McNeil needed doctoring, so here I am."

"I'm all right, Doc. It's fine."

"Well, I guess you haven't seen your face lately, Mr. McNeil," Holder said, opening his case. "It doesn't look at all fine to me, and I'm the medical professional. Hey, Jay, make yourself useful for once and fetch me some hot water and towels."

With a grimace, Lamar left his work on the door repairs and headed to the back to heat water. When he returned, Doc Holder went to work cleaning McNeil's injuries and then dabbing medicine from his case on them."

"Ouch!" McNeil said sharply.

"I know," Doc said sympathetically, but continuing his work. "It stings like anything. But I have to disinfect the cuts. That's a deep one over your right eye, too. It needs stitches."

"No, it's fine, Doc. Thanks very much."

"If you think he looks bad, Doc, you should see the other feller," Long chortled. "God almighty, I never saw a fight like that one before. I thought McNeil was going to beat that saddle bum to death. You should have seen it. Sommers and his gunslinger had to carry what McNeil left of him out of here and hoist him up in the saddle like a side of beef."

"You're both lucky to be alive," Doc said. "I can't believe Sommers stood for that."

"He wouldn't have," McNeil said, had Sam from the livery not showed up with a Winchester.

"Sam did that?" Doc said in wonderment. "He never mentioned it."

"Say, McNeil," Long said. "Where did you learn to fight like that? You hit that cowboy three or four times for every punch he landed on you, and harder."

"I did some boxing in my youth."

"Boxing? What's that?" Long said.

"It's fist fighting, Bud," Doc said, amazed sometimes by his friend's ignorance of the great big world outside Dead Horse Crossing. "Only with lots of rules."

"Well, whatever it was, it was fighting like I've never seen before."

"Your friend is pretty tough," Jay Lamar said sarcastically to Long, waving a hand at McNeil.

"Yeah, you're darn tootin'. He defends himself when attacked."

Lamar shook his head and returned to his work at the front door.

"I'll tell you something, Marshal," McNeil said.

"What's that?"

"You said once I didn't respect you, and you didn't blame me. Well, maybe there was some truth to that then. But watching you stand up to Sommers and buffaloing him into not letting Newsome shoot me was maybe the second-most courageous thing I ever saw in my entire life. Also, the second-dumbest thing I ever saw since you almost got yourself killed. But I'll tell you what, Marshal. You now have my respect and more."

"Well, I appreciate that, McNeil. But now I won't be able to sleep a wink, not knowing what the most courageous and dumbest things were you saw."

McNeil laughed a little. "That would be when Denton Everhart ran through heavy fire and fought six enemy soldiers using only a bayonet. He killed three, and when the others broke and ran, he picked me up, hoisted me onto his back, and carried me a mile to a field hospital when I was nearly shot to pieces. For all Denton knew, he risked his life to save a dead man."

"Lord almighty," Long said. "I did nothing close to that, McNeil."

"Sure you did, Marshal."

"He ain't the marshal anymore," Lamar chided. "Sommers took his badge."

"What?" Doc Holder said, noticing the star missing from his friend's shirt for the first time. "He had no right doing that."

McNeil could see Doc was as angry as it had made him seeing Sommers take Long's badge.

"It was only a hunk of tin," Long said quietly. "Let him keep it. It means nothing. And I was thinking of getting out of the marshal business, anyway." Despite the words, Long's shoulders slumped as he showed his rekindled feelings of humiliation.

"And do what?" Holder exclaimed.

"Maybe I'll become a doctor," Long said, his eyes downcast. "After all, it can't be that hard if you finished medical training."

McNeil laughed.

"You better stick with the marshal business, Bud," Holder said with some irritation. "No offense, but I think you make a better marshal than you would a doctor."

Holder finished working on McNeil and closed his case.

"Don't worry, Marshal, they haven't licked us yet," McNeil said, noticing Long's embarrassment.

"Haven't they?" Long said morosely. "I feel whipped. And I know I'm useless after letting Sommers tear that badge off my shirt."

"No man is useless as long as he's got a friend," Holder said with emotion. "And, Bud, I'm your friend."

"But now we'll never get word to those cattlemen," Long continued, his shoulders hunched. "Cotton Patrick was our only hope of that. The herd will be here the day after tomorrow or the next day. Sommers will sell them his infected cows." He raised his eyes to McNeil. "Not to mention, he'll probably ride in here with his crew tomorrow and kill both of us. Then he will have won the whole shebang."

"Let's take things a day at a time," McNeil said quietly. "Thinking that way will not get us anywhere."

"You know something, McNeil. You should pack up your kit and ride out of this town while you still can. Sommers doesn't have the men to do more than maybe watch the main road north and south. You could ride straight east or west across country for a day and then turn whichever way you pleased. You don't owe this town anything, and you have nothing to prove to anyone."

"Except maybe to myself. The first day I got here, I thought maybe I could put my gun away, settle down in a place like this, and get a little piece of land and raise some cattle. Not around here, of course, but a place where folks are friendly." McNeil grinned for a moment but then turned serious again. "Someplace where people didn't know me, and my reputation wouldn't work against me. But now I know I can't do that. A self-important, moneyed tyrant who thinks the law doesn't apply to him killed my friend. Maybe two of my friends. I was warming up to that rawboned cowpuncher, Patrick. I couldn't look myself in the mirror again if I lit a shuck out of here and let that go."

"I guess I understand what you're saying," Long said.

"It's clear as day, Bud," Doc Holder said. "He is saying there comes a time when a man has just got to do something if he intends to keep calling himself a man."

Long sighed and ran a thick hand over his forehead. "I've got such a headache. I hurt all over, and I'm bewildered."

"I get bewildered sometimes," McNeil said. "Sometimes I feel like I can't tell up from down."

Long sighed again. "Don't worry, Mr. McNeil. I'm not quittin' on you. I guess I just needed a minute to feel sorry for myself."

"Don't you fret about it, Bud. We'll get your badge back. Now go home and get some sleep. And as your physician, that's an order. Things won't look so bleak when the sun rises in the morning."

"Okay, Doc," Long said. "Maybe you're right, for once." Then he turned and shuffled out the door.

Chapter 21

Self-Reflection

McNeil sat in a chair in front of the hotel, sipping coffee from a tin cup. Resolved not to make the same mistake again that had nearly cost him his life the previous evening, he wore the tied-down Colt on his hip. Only a crazy man made the same mistake twice. After the doings in the hotel lobby the night before, McNeil had no intention of appearing in public unarmed again until the looming confrontation with Sommers ended.

Jay Lamar sat in the chair beside him. The hotel clerk behaved almost cordially toward McNeil and had volunteered to brew coffee that morning for the first time since McNeil had checked in. It appeared to McNeil that Lamar had something on his mind and wished to talk, but hadn't yet thought of a way to start the conversation. McNeil didn't prod the man. He already had enough on his mind without worrying about Lamar's troubles.

McNeil wasn't the name he had been born with, nor the name he carried when he first traveled west. Instead, he had been born with a fine Irish name. But unfortunately, McNeil had been on the wrong side of things during his youth, especially where law and order were concerned. The horrors of the war and the indignities imposed on those who had borne arms against the Union had left a foul taste in McNeil's mouth. Unfortunately, he had responded to those angry feelings with violent and often vengeful actions.

Blessed with superior hand-eye coordination, McNeil was always fast on the draw and deadly accurate. Soon, in cattle towns from Kansas to New Mexico to Colorado, he had gained a reputation as a man not to be trifled with, a killer. His name became a legend throughout the plains country, a fighting man good with his fists but whose skill with a Colt was comparable to that of gunmen like Hickok, Hardin, and Earp. Even the lawmen he encountered left him alone. But with age came wisdom.

Trouble-hunting men who wanted to prove how tough and fast they were, had sought him out, looking to make a name for themselves. Tired of the killing and knowing inevitably he would someday encounter a man a fraction of a second faster and get killed, McNeil drifted to south Texas. He became a man fleeing from a reputation, the reputation of a killer fast on the draw. He had changed his name many times over the years. But it seemed there was always some chance meeting with trouble he couldn't avoid—another encounter with some trouble-hunting stranger with something to prove.

McNeil had been fortunate that few men knew him well and most descriptions of him were wildly inaccurate. But with every gun battle, someone would witness McNeil's skill with a gun and associate him with a noted gunman they had heard of in the past. Each such incident forced another name change and would set McNeil drifting once again.

"I'm truly worried about my sister, Kate," Lamar said finally.

"You've no idea where she's gone?" McNeil said. "After the incident the night before, he had discounted Bud Long's theory that Sommers might hold the woman hostage to use as leverage. Instead, he was as mystified by Kate's disappearance as her brother.

"Now that you're back here at the hotel, I realize you aren't holding her somewhere," Lamar said.

"Kate left Doc's place the other day without a word. That's the sum of my knowledge about her disappearance."

"Sometimes, when we argued, Kate would threaten to leave for Denver or someplace back east," Lamar said.

"But everyone says she loves this town," McNeil said. "That she would do anything to save it, including going along with Sommers' plan."

"That's not true, exactly," Lamar said. "Kate never loved this town. She loves me and knows I'd never leave Dead Horse Crossing. And Kate knows I'm too weak to make a go of it alone."

"Then maybe she left when it seemed someone might derail Sommers' plan."

"You ought to do yourself a favor and ride on while you still got time to do it," Lamar said.

"Can't do that. Those that killed my friends must answer for their deeds."

"You're only going to get yourself killed, you know. And Bud Long too, it appears, since he's taken your side in this. But Sommers will have too many men."

"Why, Jay? Are you worried about me getting killed all of a sudden?"

"I don't like to see any man murdered, that's all. You should have never come here."

"I'm inclined to agree with you. But I did, and here I must stay for a while longer."

"I don't want to get involved."

"Involved in what?"

"Whatever will happen when Sommers and his men come to town. I've got to go on living here. These people are my neighbors, my friends."

"All of them?"

"This is my town, McNeil, like it or not. Whatever happened here happened and you can't be undo it. It's—it's—"

"Dead and buried? You don't seem to like what happened here much. Why stick around? Maybe you should have gone with your sister."

"What do you care? You care nothing about Dead Horse Crossing."

"No, not much. But this much I know. The rule of law has been suspended here, and evil has taken over."

"You're a fine one to talk. You came here and aim to kill folks."

"I didn't come here for that purpose, Jay. But I won't deny it. Yes, after what I've learned, I aim to kill those who killed my friends. The same people who aim to kill me. Sometimes you must ride the vengeance trail, whether that's what you want or isn't. Am I wrong, Jay?"

McNeil sipped his coffee, now growing cold, as Jay Lamar struggled to formulate an answer. But the man couldn't find an answer.

Bud Long walked up the steps to the boardwalk and leaned on a post supporting the porch overhang. "Saw you were around and thought I'd give you the news," he said to McNeil.

"I'm around all right. What news?"

"I was at the post office. Since I'm no longer the marshal, but just another layabout, Beeson figured it was okay to tell me. The herd will arrive tomorrow evening. The trail boss sent the wire."

McNeil nodded. "We still might spoil Sommers' plans yet, if he acts today or tomorrow morning. I can't feature him wanting to leave anyone alive who might tell those cattlemen about the anthrax breakout. But I'd hoped Patrick would reach them so that the trail boss would have wired they weren't coming. I thought if that happened, then maybe Sommers would let things alone."

"Well, I think we're well past that, anyway. I think it's personal with Sommers now, and he feels he has to kill you to show he's still boss. So today or tomorrow morning, he'll come."

"Let him come," McNeil said. "Sommers is about to learn the price of doing murder has gone up."

Chapter 22

The Herd

Phil Anderson, the trail scout for the Goodnight-Loving herd bound for Denver, rode northeast. He decided when he drew even with the knob up ahead that he would bear in a more easterly direction to search for an alternative place to cross the Pecos. Anderson disliked deviating from the established trail with the dependable grass for the herd. But given the news of anthrax among the cattle in Dead Horse Crossing, they must give the place a wide berth.

Charlie Goodnight and Oliver Loving hadn't been happy when the trail boss had wired them the news. There was about five thousand head in the herd when the drive left south Texas, and the men and their investors had planned to add at least another fifteen hundred head to the tally at Dead Horse Crossing, paying half the price they would get for the cattle in Denver. But they had much appreciated learning of the anthrax breakout before it was too late. It was far better for the drive to arrive in Denver with the five thousand head they started with than not at all. Anderson shuddered at the thought of what would have happened had they added the infected cows to the herd. He still marveled at the grit of the young rider from Dead Horse Crossing who had traveled alone over rough country day and night to bring them the news.

Something ahead caught Anderson's attention before he reached the small hill. First, he saw two riderless but saddled ponies grazing with no one about. Then he saw the vultures. Anderson urged his horse to increase the pace but kept the animal under a gallop to not spook the two horses. Then, as he drew closer, he saw what had attracted the vultures. Three men lay dead on the trail. When Anderson dismounted, he saw an awful sight. Coyotes, vultures, and who knew what else had been at the bodies for a while. Pulling his bandana up over his nose and mouth to cut the smell, he ambled in a circle around the bodies, trying to work out what had happened.

Two men lay close together, their pistols in their holsters as if they had ridden up together and dismounted from their horses. The third, however, lay face down with his Colt just beyond his outstretched hand. The large hole in the man's back was as near as Anderson could tell, the exit wound from a bullet fired from a rifle. Maybe the two men had shot the third from ambush but hadn't killed him right off. Then, when they rode up to check their handiwork, he had killed them both for their trouble before he died. Then Anderson noticed the two smaller holes in the back of the third man's cotton shirt. Those looked to be from pistol shots. But they had bled only a little. Anderson figured the man had already died before someone shot him with the pistol. It was the rifle bullet that killed him.

Anderson scooped up the Colt, opened the loading gate, and rotated the cylinder. The young cowboy had fired four times. He saw someone, probably the owner, had carved the initials "CP" into the wood handle on one side of the Colt. Anderson stuck the pistol into the front of his gun belt. Then he walked slowly to the grazing horses whose reins trailed along the ground. Speaking to them in soothing tones, he caught them both with ease. A scabbard on the saddle of one horse held a Winchester. Anderson pulled it out and sniffed the barrel. Sure enough, someone had fired it recently.

"Well, pard," Anderson said, looking at the face down cowboy. "Looks like you at least killed those two varmints who ambushed you on the trail."

It seemed a dead man had killed those two hombres before knowing he was dead. Putting the rifle back in the sheath, Anderson led the horses to his mount and stepped into his saddle. Then he turned and galloped back to the herd with the two horses in tow to report his findings to Wesley Cole, the trail boss.

∼ele∼

Wesley Cole, Phil Anderson, the rider from Dead Horse Crossing, and two drovers stood a little distance away from the three bodies, taking in the grisly scene. As the group started forward, Anderson grabbed the young rider's arm.

"I'd wait here with the horses, were I you. It's not a pretty sight. The coyotes, vultures, and such have been at those boys for a while now."

"Thanks for your concern, but I might know them if they are from my town."

"They are long past anyone recognizing them."

"Still, I wish to look."

"Suit yourself," Anderson said, removing his hand.

As the group approached the dead men with their bandanas pulled up, the rider pointed to the two men lying close together.

"I'm sure that one is Red Smith, a cowhand from the Bar Deuce," the rider said. "They called him Smitty. I can tell from his hair. But I can't say about the one beside him. Probably another Bar Deuce hand."

"What about the other one?" Cole said.

"That's Cotton Patrick, a friend of mine," the rider said. "I recognize the spurs. He was always proud of them. And those are his initials on the Colt Mr. Anderson found beside him."

Cole nodded and turned to the drovers. "Take those spades, boys, and bury what's left of them. It's the least we can do."

"Mr. Cole," the rider said. "I know it's a big favor to ask, but I'd like to take Cotton back to Dead Horse Crossing. He deserves a decent burial. But the other two skunks deserve what they get, unmarked graves beside a cow trail."

Cole nodded and said, "I understand. When the herd gets here, we'll wrap him up in some canvas and put him in the hooligan wagon." Then, turning to Anderson, Cole said, "Phil, you better get going and find us an alternate crossing point at the Pecos. If you're not back when the herd gets here, I'll have the boys hold them."

"Okay, boss," Anderson said. Then, after tipping his hat to the rider, he caught his horse, climbed aboard, and rode away."

"You've been very kind, Mr. Cole," the rider said. "I can pack Cotton back to town on one of the horses Mr. Anderson found and caught. It's only about another eight hours to town from here."

"A couple of the men and I will accompany you back to Dead Horse Crossing once we get the herd across the Pecos. After that, I'll turn my duties over to my segundo until we can rejoin the herd."

"That's unnecessary. I don't want to trouble you to do that. I can make it back to town alone."

"From what I've seen of you, I'm sure you can make it back safely alone. But I'm interested in the man you described and the circumstances he's facing in your town."

"Mr. McNeil?"

Cole nodded. "He sounds mighty familiar to me, though I don't know him by the name McNeil. Still, the man sounds like someone who used to work for me some years ago. And if it's him, I'd like to stop that rancher from killing him if we can get there in time."

Cole and the rider moved upwind of the bodies while the drovers labored to dig the graves.

"Care to speculate on what these three were doing here?" Cole said. "I think Anderson is right. Those two probably shot your friend from atop that little knob there. And then when they rode over to him, he had the sand to live long enough to plug them both when they stepped down from their saddles. One thing is for sure. Your friend died real good."

"I expect Cotton was trying to reach you and the herd to warn you as I did," the rider said. "He tied up with McNeil right before I left. But I told no one where I was going when I left, so they wouldn't have known I was already on the way with the warning. And, I suppose Sommers sent those men to stop him."

"Maybe you should have shared your plans before leaving your town," Cole said. "Might have saved that young cowboy's life."

"I know, and I'm powerfully sorry about Cotton. But if I'd told them, they would have prevented me from doing what I did. You know how it is, Mr. Cole. No one expects too much from a woman. All they expect from us is to look pretty and be able to cook a decent meal. Well, that's not enough. Maybe I can't do everything as well as a man because I lack the muscle. But there are things like riding and shooting a rifle that I can do better than most any man I've ever met. They would never have let me bring the warning alone because they wouldn't have expected I could do it. That's why I didn't tell them."

"Well, it looks like you showed them, Miss Lamar. And you've got sand. I'll give you that. So maybe they will learn from what you've done to expect a little more from you in the future."

Chapter 23

A Dangerous Man

SOMMERS WAS AT HIS desk at the Bar Deuce ranch house, updating the cattle tally ledger. Finally, the wire from the herd's trail boss had come through, and he knew when the herd would arrive. Despite the heavy losses to anthrax, he felt confident he could supply the fifteen hundred head the contract called for, assuming the losses continued to decline. Someone pounded on the front door.

"Come in," Sommers bellowed.

Grover Rhodes entered, hat in hand.

"How does it look this morning, Grover?"

"The boys found about thirty dead beeves on the west range this morning. I've got three of them rounding up and burning the carcasses. The rest of the men moved the healthy cows down to the south range."

"That's not great news, but at least the numbers continue to decline. So maybe the disease has about run its course."

Rhodes nodded. "It appears we'll have no trouble supplying the fifteen hundred head you promised to deliver."

"How many hands do we have left after the desertions?"

"Eight, with Len Johnson back on his feet. Nine counting me."

"I'd feel better having a few more along to take care of our problem in town. Is Fitz back from town yet?"

"No, I haven't seen him. I figured he is attending to his new marshal duties."

"In a way, he is. With Fitz as town marshal, it will put the law and order stamp of approval on what we must do to solve our problem. That should keep any outside lawmen out of our business. So the townsfolk need to see Fitz in town doing his duty. But I also told him to check the saloon for the layabouts that quit. Maybe some haven't hired on with another outfit or left the country. I'm hoping he can scrounge up a few more guns to accompany us to town."

"I'm not worried about it," Rhodes said. "That broken-down old drunk, Bud Long, won't be a problem. We've only one man to worry about."

"Well, after watching him take Johnson apart piece by piece at the hotel, I find him more formidable than before."

"Don't worry, boss, I'll take care of McNeil. The whole thing will be over in three minutes unless they hide, and we have to find them before we kill them."

"While I can't know what McNeil intends to do, I think it's safe to say that man will not hide. Had I known killing Denton Everhart would draw a man like McNeil to this town, I might have handled that situation differently. The man's a distraction I don't need."

"He won't be a distraction much longer. So, when are we going to take care of him?"

"First thing tomorrow morning. That leaves the rest of the day to move the cattle to the rendezvous with those trail drivers. Then we'll make the delivery, and I'll get my money."

"I only hope none of our cattle die on them until that herd is well away from Bar Deuce range. Those drovers might come back looking to reclaim their money."

"All I need is a day's head start. As soon as I've got that money in hand, I'm getting out of the cattle business for a spell. I'm heading back east until it all blows over. I'm missing the comforts of a more civilized climate, anyway."

"You will leave a bunch of angry folks behind, boss. The ranchers who contributed cattle to the roundup will be angry when they learn you've absconded with their money. The townsfolk will be upset when there is no cash to get them through until next year. And our hands are all going to find themselves out of work. People who feel cheated have long memories."

"I can't take responsibility for the world's problems, Grover. I've got plenty of my own. Anthrax has cut my profits to the bone on this deal. And I'm taking care of you as we agreed, so you have nothing to kick about."

"Oh, I'm with you, boss—one hundred percent. As long as I get mine, I'm happy. I'm thinking about heading down to south Texas, and I won't have a problem finding an outfit there to tie up with."

The door opened, and Fitz Newsome breezed into the room. His habit of walking into the ranch house without knocking irritated Sommers to no end. But knowing the man's propensity toward violence, Sommers knew better than to make an issue of it.

"Did you have any luck?"

"I found two of the boys that quit on us. They're broke and agreed to come back. So I sent them to the bunkhouse."

"Finally, some good news," Sommers said with a satisfied smile. That gives us an even dozen counting me when we ride into town tomorrow morning."

"You're taking part, boss?" Rhodes said with surprise.

"I wouldn't miss it, Grover. I want to see it."

"I also learned something interesting at the saloon, Sommers," Newsome said.

"What's that?" Sommers said, boiling inside that Newsome never showed him proper respect as head of the outfit. But he swallowed his rage.

"I talked to a feller who has seen McNeil struttin' around town. He says he doubts that's the man's name. This feller says McNeil reminds him of someone he knew of up in Dodge City years ago."

"Reminds him of who?"

"Ian Murphy."

Sommers blanched with horror. "Ian Murphy? I heard Murphy died in a duel up in Montana Territory."

"I've heard the rumor but never believed it," Newsome said. "There was another rumor he changed his name and drifted here to Texas, down south somewhere. But, no, after talking to that feller in the saloon, I suppose I'd bet a month's pay that McNeil is Ian Murphy in the flesh."

"What does it matter what his name is?" Rhodes blustered. "He will be dead all the same."

"It matters, you ignorant wretch, because Ian Murphy is one of the most dangerous men that's ever been in the west. He's killed over twenty men, maybe even thirty, by some accounts. They say he's faster than Hardin and just as mean."

"McNeil wouldn't even fight me fairly when I challenged him," Rhodes said. "He can't be Murphy."

"That's the only part I can't figure," Newsome admitted. "Murphy isn't known for having a charitable disposition. So I can't understand why he beaned you with his gun barrel instead of just killing you. But if he is Murphy, I'd say you're about the luckiest man alive."

"I don't care what the man's name is. I aim to kill him."

Newsome laughed roundly. "Kill him? You? Not unless you catch him with his back turned the way he got the bulge on you at Kate's place. You better check your hole card, Grover."

"I told you he didn't fight me fair. Instead, he grabbed my wrist when I tried to draw and bashed my skull."

"And that took more skill and speed than he would have spent just drilling you with his Colt, you fool. You wouldn't have cleared leather."

"Well, I ain't worried about McNeil or whatever his name is."

"You can't go foolin' about with a man like him, even if he isn't Murphy. I told you he's pure poison, and he's lightning fast. Maybe you should let me take him."

"No, I won't," Rhodes said stubbornly. "The boss said I get the first crack at the man. If he beats me, which he won't, he's your meat. But not before."

"It's your funeral," Newsome said with a grin. "But if you want my advice, pull your pistol and hide it behind your back before you walk up if you don't want to get killed."

"Maybe you would like to see how fast I am, Newsome," Rhodes growled, offended by the big man's manner. His hand dropped near the butt of his gun.

Newsome grinned, but his eyes grew hard. "All right, Rhodes. I'll accommodate you." The gunman's hands dropped near the butts of his twin Colts.

"Stop this, men, right now," Sommers exclaimed. "I won't have it. Do you two want to prove how tough you are? Well, do it on your own time after we take care of the problem in town. Not before. Afterward, you can kill each other if you're a mind to."

"Whatever you say, boss," Rhodes said, secretly relieved Sommers had intervened.

"I'll let it go this time," Newsome said. "But you ever brace me like that again, Rhodes, and I'll kill you." The big man turned on his heel and left the ranch house.

"That was stupid, Grover," Sommers said. "Stupid. Fitz Newsome is a killer."

"I've taken my scalps," Grover said defensively.

"Not from men like that or Ian Murphy. I hope Newsome is wrong about that. We have to be careful in the morning, Grover. Take him down fast and get it over with."

"I said I'll take care of him, boss. And I will. Wait and see."

Chapter 24

Calm Before the Storm

A THUNDERSTORM THAT SWEPT through the Pecos country overnight had dropped torrential rains on the town of Dead Horse Crossing. The rains had turned the dirt main street into a quagmire of mud. Instead of making his way home in the pouring rain the previous evening, Bud Long had taken a room at the hotel and passed the night there. Doc Holder called at the hotel at seven o'clock in the morning to find McNeil, Long, and Jay Lamar in the lobby.

"Well, it sure came a gully washer last night," Holder chortled. "A real frog-strangler. The street out there is nothing but a big mud hole. But at least the sun is out now, and the rain washed all the dust out of the air. It looks like we will get a nice day today."

"Yeah, it looks like it will be a pretty day to set things right," Bud Long agreed.

"Well, enjoy it while you can," McNeil said. "The day will get ugly soon enough."

"When you figure they'll come, McNeil?"

"Maybe an hour, two at the most. The herd gets in this afternoon. They will want to finish us early, so they have time to drive their cows to the rendezvous with the herd."

"Sounds about right."

"You keep that messenger gun close, Marshal."

"I always liked me a weapon with a little heft to it."

"It's a darn good weapon for the kind of close work we have ahead of us. When they get here, we're going to kill every one of them."

"For two men on open ground drawing from a cold deck, you sure have a lot of killing in mind, son. Is that still your plan? We're still meeting them out there in the street?"

"I haven't changed it, Marshal. I reckon it's the best way for us to go about it. So you best get your mind around what has to be done. Men will die here today. And we're going to kill them."

"It seems to me it would be better for you and Bud to shoot at them from cover," Doc Holder said.

"No, it wouldn't. We do that, and they would surround us and kill us one by one. We will walk right up to them, and I'll say my piece. While they are chewing my words over in their minds, we'll commence killing them. That should unnerve them a little. It ain't much, but it's all the advantage we're going to get."

Jay Lamar brought over a tray with coffee cups and passed it around.

"It's a shame what this town and the people in it have come to," Doc Holder said, looking pointedly at Lamar as he took a cup from the tray. "You could do something about it, Jay."

"Like what? I'm just a hotel clerk."

"You're a man, ain't you?"

"I'm not standing against Sommers and his men just to get killed for my trouble."

"I know you're scared, Jay. So am I. I'm petrified."

"Lemme alone, Doc, will you?"

"There's some things worse than dying, Jay. Sommers killed Denton Everhart, and none of us even said a word about it. Now he's on his way here to kill this man and Bud, too. When will it stop?"

"Lemme alone, I tell you!" Lamar exclaimed.

"I can't let you alone. I can't let myself alone. Don't you understand that?"

The muscles around Lamar's mouth tightened. Then, self-consciously, he retreated to the front desk with his coffee cup, shutting his ears to Holder's words.

"Funny how a man clings to the earth when he faces death," Bud Long said with sadness. "Makes it easier to justify rolling over instead of fighting back."

"There's a difference between clinging to the earth," Holder said, eyeing Lamar across the lobby with contempt, "and crawling on it with your belly in the dirt."

"I ain't gettin' into it, and that's that," Lamar exclaimed.

Holder sighed and looked at McNeil. "Maybe you better give me that Walker Colt back. I know I won't account for much, but maybe I can do something."

McNeil shook his head. "No, Doc. People will need you once the gun smoke clears. The marshal and I will do what killing needs doing. You stick to your doctoring." Then, turning to Bud Long, he said, "Marshal, I better get that extra Winchester and ammunition stashed over at the livery where we can get to it later. Time is growing short."

Long nodded, getting up. "I'll trail along with you."

Chapter 25

Riding to Town

BULL SOMMERS, GROVER RHODES, and Fitz Newsome stood before the assembled ranch hands. Sommers sensed his men were full of anxious thoughts. None of them, except Rhodes and Newsome, were looking forward to what they faced. They were cowpunchers, not gunmen. A few of them maybe had traded gunfire with would-be rustlers at various times, but always at a distance with pistols so that none of them had ever expected to kill or get killed. It had only been a little excitement to break up the usual monotony of ranch work.

The ranch hands were all young men, too young to have taken part in the big war. None had even done any soldiering against the Indians. Sommers had watched the country change much over the past two decades. And from his perspective, not always for good. The Indian Wars in Texas had ended with Colonel Mackenzie's defeat of the Comanches and Quanah Parker, the tribe's half-white war chief. Cattle had replaced the buffalo on the staked plains. Still, the land from which the white man had driven the Comanche had not yet found peace. Men still rode with guns at hand, just as he and his men would do this day. Sommers addressed his men.

"You have nothing to worry about, men," he said. "The numbers are stacked in our favor, and we shouldn't have more than a few minutes' work to do in town. Afterward, we'll ride back here and drive the cattle to the rendezvous with the herd coming in this afternoon."

"Is a true, Mr. Sommers?" one cowboy called from the back.

"Is what true?"

"Is it true that man in town, the one whose hide you're after, is Ian Murphy?"

Sommers heard the name repeated in murmurs within the group.

"We don't know that," Sommers said. "That's only speculation, and it doesn't matter one whit, anyway. We're after one man, and there are twelve of us standing here."

"I just don't cotton to the idea of going against a killer like Murphy," another cowboy said.

"You'll do what the boss says," Rhodes bellowed. "Any man that doesn't will answer to me."

"Shut up, Grover," Sommers whispered angrily. "Threats will not encourage them."

"You men know me," Fitz Newsome bellowed. "It doesn't matter if McNeil is Ian Murphy or not. I aim to kill him, and I intend to shoulder the bulk of the load. So you boys only have to worry about the light work. You ought to pray it is him, then someday you can brag to your grandchildren you added a bullet to the corpse of Ian Murphy."

Rhodes swiveled his head toward Newsome, throwing the haughty gunman a baleful stare. He made up his mind that he would kill Newsome if the man interfered with his play in town against McNeil.

Sommers shook his head, hoping Rhodes and Newsome settled their private animosity after they had killed McNeil. Then, turning back to the ranch hands, he bellowed, "Saddle up and check your guns, men. We ride to town in ten minutes."

———❦———

Ten minutes later, Sommers and his men rode out of the ranch yard at the Bar Deuce, saddle leather creaking and bridles jingling. Sommers and Rhodes rode at the head of the column of twos. Newsome had taken a position at the back of the line. He would deal with any cowpoke who might decide to cut and run. The riders moved along with their horses at a trot. Steel-shod hooves tossed up chunks of wet earth as the men rode along the muddy road toward Dead Horse Crossing.

Charlie Watson, the man riding beside Fitz Newsome at the back of the column, thought back to a night in an El Paso saloon. He had been nineteen. Another cowhand who had drunk too much whiskey interpreted some foolish thing Watson had said as an insult. The man had challenged Watson to draw. Watson had been so scared he almost wet himself, but the only thing he'd feared more than death that night was others thinking him a coward. So, he had stood up on shaky legs. It had turned out that the men matched up fairly. Both palmed their six guns almost simultaneously, the other only slightly faster. Watson had got lucky. Thanks to the whiskey, the other cowboy's shot missed him while Watson's aim had been true. That experience had taught Watson one thing. Fast was good, but accuracy was deadly.

Minutes later, a lawman showed up and disarmed him. Men carried the dead man to the undertaker, and Watson spent a night in the town jail. The next morning, the lawman told Watson it seemed it had been a fair shooting. He gave Watson his pistol back and then invited him to leave El Paso and not come back.

Watson had never forgotten that night, especially the man lying on that sawdust-covered saloon floor with a bullet hole in his chest. Watson had been far more careful with his speech and had stayed out of saloons from that day forward. As far as he knew, except for Rhodes and Newsome, he was the only man among the Bar Deuce crew who had ever killed a man in a stand-up gunfight. Watson knew he wasn't looking forward to tangling with that man in town, no matter who he was. He figured the rest of the boys felt the same, only stronger. But like cowboys throughout the land, they all took their responsibility to ride for the brand seriously. And not one of them wanted anyone thinking of him as yellow.

Chapter 26

Waiting

Kate Lamar watched the drovers pull the canvas-wrapped, rope-bound body of Cotton Patrick from the wagon. The men carried their burden to the waiting unsaddled pony and carefully laid the body over the horse's back. Then they tied the corpse securely on the horse.

The trail drivers had moved the herd across the Pecos at the alternate shallow crossing Phil Anderson had found. Wesley Cole gave his assistant trail boss last-minute instructions.

"We won't be gone long, but don't wait," he said. "Get the herd moving north. Then, swing back west after two miles until you strike the trail again. You'll be well past the town by then."

"Okay, boss."

"The boys and I will catch up with you after we see what's what in that town."

Cole's segundo nodded and strolled away to give his orders to the rest of the crew.

"Let's get riding," Cole said to those standing around him. "We should make Dead Horse Crossing by nine o'clock. I hope we'll make it in time."

Cole, Phil Anderson, Kate Lamar, and two other drovers climbed onto their horses, and Cole led them west toward town. Kate held the reins of the pony, carrying her friend Cotton.

—ele—

It was approaching eight-fifteen when Sommers' cavalcade reached the outskirts of Dead Horse Crossing. No one was moving on the street ahead. It seemed everyone in town knew a fight was coming and had taken shelter in their homes. The riders rode on with their mounts at a steady trot, with grim faces.

—ele—

"Morning, Sam," Bud Long said to the grizzled old liveryman.

Sam paused his work and leaned on the handle of a pitchfork.

"Good day to you, Marshal. You too, young feller."

"Morning, Sam," McNeil said. "I never had the chance to thank you for the other night. So, much obliged to you for taking a hand in that game over at the hotel."

"Don't mention it, son. Unlike some in this town, I've never been partial to Sommers' ways or his gun hands, either."

"We would like to place this rifle and ammunition in your barn so we can get to it later," McNeil said. "We'll try to keep the fight out of your barn, but I can't promise we'll be able to."

"Help yourself, and I already moved the stock outside to the corral, so you won't hurt a thing being in here if you need a place to hole up." Then the liveryman pointed up at the hayloft. "I'll be up there with my old Winchester, and I'll help you fellers the best I can."

"Appreciate the offer," McNeil said. "But we don't want to get any innocent folks shot up."

"Don't you worry about me, young feller," Sam cackled. "The Comanches were still raidin' when I come up. I've been in a shootin' scrape a time or two and know how to keep my head down."

"All right, just be careful, Sam."

Sam nodded. "I'll be wishin' you both luck."

"Thank you. We'll need all we can get," Long chuckled.

After stowing the rifle and ammunition, McNeil followed Bud Long back across the street, balancing on the planks someone had thrown down to make a path over the mud. They sat down on the boardwalk in the chairs out front of the hotel to wait. The other Winchester leaned against the wall next to McNeil's chair, and Bud Long had the scattergun across his legs.

"You see to your guns, Marshal?"

"Yeah, I'm loaded for bear. And I had sense enough to load firearms with no reminder long before I ever met you, McNeil." Then the man laughed good-naturedly to show he meant no offense.

"I expect so," McNeil said. "I'm probably just rattling on because of the nerves. Waitin' is always the hardest part of it."

"You all right, McNeil?" Long said, surprised the man had admitted to nervousness.

"I'm fine. I've got no problem with killing. Never have."

"It's just I never expected that you, you know—"

"Get nervous, Marshal? Well, that's part of it, I guess. Mostly, it's because I have some old feelings surfacing. You all right, Marshal?"

"I'm as right as a man can be under present circumstances. Just a little jumpy, I guess. And maybe a little bit scared."

Long went quiet for a couple of beats.

"I've never asked you any questions, McNeil. But some things you've said the past couple of days sounded curious. Like there is some history to go with them."

"I killed my first man when I was seventeen at a place called Gaines' Mill during the war. My pa took me hunting and taught me how to shoot as a youngster. In the war, I found out I was as good at killing men as wild game. The army was glad to have me. After the war, I learned how to draw a pistol fast and shoot it accurately. So, it wasn't long after I came west that I was killing men not wearing uniforms. The first was a card cheat in Abilene at the end of a trail drive. But it wasn't long after I made myself a reputation that men who thought they might be faster sought me out, wanting to try their skills against the man many folks said was one of the best."

"I figured all along that your name might not be McNeil," Long said. "I'd hate going to my maker today, not knowing your true name."

McNeil stared woodenly out across the street for several long moments. "Ian Patrick Murphy is the name my ma and pa gave me when I was born. I've had several names since while trying to leave my reputation behind. McNeil seems a good name, so I use it."

"Sorry for prying. Just an old man's curiosity. Your past is your business."

"Well, now you know, Marshal. I'm sure you've heard the name being a lawman and all. But now, I'll ask you to forget it as a favor. Ian Murphy is a past I don't plan to return to, and far as I know, the law doesn't want me for anything. But I don't mind you knowing my true name. If you live out the day and I don't, I guess I'd like him to carve my good Irish name on the marker when the undertaker plants me in the graveyard outside town."

"Hey, Marshal!" someone shouted.

McNeil and Long looked up at the open loft door of the livery across the street. They saw Sam crouched in the doorway, waving his arms at them. When the man saw he had their attention, he held his hands with all ten fingers extended. Then he held up one hand with two fingers extended.

"Looks like an even dozen coming," McNeil said flatly.

"That's a lot of guns."

"Could have been a lot worse," McNeil said.

Long dug into a shirt pocket and pulled out two cigars. He offered one to McNeil, who took it.

"I always get a hankerin' for a good smoke this time of morning," Long said. He nipped the end off the cigar with his teeth and put it in his mouth. McNeil did the same. Long fetched a match from another pocket and struck it on the side of the chair. Then he lit McNeil's cigar before lighting his own. The men sat and smoked in silence for several moments.

"Soon as they show at the head of the street, we'll walk down to meet them. They will dismount and line up when they see us. Remember, Marshal, don't stop. Once we start, keep moving forward. We'll walk right up on them. When I'm ready, I will shout a quick question at Rhodes. I expect he'll answer me.

And then I'll open the ball. So, when you hear me ask the question, that's your sign. You start right in on Newsome with that coach gun. Then do the rest, just like we planned."

"I sure hate walking down that street, getting my boots all muddy."

"Don't worry, Marshal. You'll forget the mud soon enough. You will have plenty of other things to occupy your mind."

Chapter 27

A Reckoning Begins

IT SURPRISED SOMMERS WHEN he saw McNeil and Bud Long striding down the middle of the muddy street toward them. Their audacity unnerved him a little. Bud Long had a messenger gun in his hands, and McNeil walked with a Winchester tucked in the crook of his left arm with the muzzle pointed at the ground. Sommers shouted to the men to dismount. The riders peeled off to opposite sides of the street, climbed down, and tied their horses to the hitching rails or posts.

"Line up," Sommers bellowed, jerking his Winchester from the saddle scabbard.

The men fell into line much like they had ridden into town, spread out six abreast in two ranks. The cowhands in the back took some comfort in standing behind, shielded by the first row of men.

Sommers and Rhodes stood in the middle. Two cowpunchers were on Sommers' left and Grover Rhodes stood next to him on his right. Fitz Newsome stood on the right side of Rhodes with a third ranch hand next to Newsome at the right end of the line. The other six cowpunchers formed the second rank, Charlie Watson among them.

"It seems funny," Bud Long stuttered to McNeil. "My mouth is wet, and my hands are dry. You would think it would be the other way around."

McNeil made no reply as the men continued slogging forward through the mud toward Sommers and his men.

"Hold fast," Sommers barked. "Let them come to us, men, if that's how they want it. Grover, take McNeil as soon as they stop walking."

But McNeil and Long kept coming. Without pausing a beat, McNeil looked directly at Grover Rhodes and shouted, "You the one who killed my friend Denton Everhart?"

The question caught Rhodes unawares, but without thinking, he sneered back, "That's right. I shot Cotton Patrick, too. And I enjoyed it."

Rhodes hadn't even reached for his pistol when he saw McNeil, still walking, pulling his Colt in a blur and thumbing back the hammer. McNeil shot him dead in the forehead. With bulging eyes and a look of disbelief, Grover Rhodes sank to his knees and fell over on his side. At almost the same instant McNeil shot Rhodes, Long's scattergun boomed.

Bud Long had been so nervous he had accidentally cocked both hammers of the ten gauge William Moore & Company coach gun. So when he pulled the first trigger, the recoil caused him to pull the second almost simultaneously, but his aim was true. The fan of buckshot from both barrels struck Fitz Newsome in the center of his belt buckle, and the force of the blast sent his legs flying straight out behind him. From Bud Long's perspective, time had ground to a halt. He heard nothing, felt nothing, tasted nothing, and smelled nothing. His sight seemed to be his only functioning sense. In fascination, he watched the surreal image of Newsome seeming to float suspended horizontally in the air for an instant before his body hit the muddy street face down.

After shooting Grover Rhodes, McNeil cocked and swung his pistol to the right to shoot Sommers. But the cowboy who stood on the right end of the line snapped a shot at McNeil that whizzed past his face, barely missing his nose. Unfortunately, that spoiled McNeil's aim, so the bullet he had intended for Sommers' chest instead hit the rancher in the right shoulder. Sommers yelped, dropped the Winchester he had been carrying, and sat down. Then, thumbing the hammer of the Colt, McNeil pivoted to his left and shot the cowboy in the face who had fired at him. The bullet took the cowboy just above his upper lip. The man's blood and brains splattered the face of the cowpuncher standing behind him. That man screamed in horror and then, clawing at his face, turned and ran away up the street. McNeil aimed at the center of the running man's back, but Ian Murphy shot no man in the back, so instead, he pivoted and swung the Colt back to his right, seeking to finish Sommers. Bud Long, not nearly as particular about where he shot men who had come to kill him, had long since discarded the empty scattergun and pulled his Schofield top-break revolver. He aimed at the back of the fleeing cowboy and shot him dead.

Sommers had not only got up but was a good way up the street and still running toward the dry goods store. McNeil snapped a shot at him but missed. The two cowboys who had been on Sommers' left at the start were shooting wildly at McNeil. But even at near point-blank range, both kept missing. McNeil calmly shifted his Colt to them from the fleeing Sommers and shot them both.

All six of the ranch hands in the second rank had turned, scattered like a covey of quail, and sought cover when the shooting started. They had ducked behind watering troughs, building corners, and in some cases, their tied horses. Most were shooting down the street toward Long and McNeil, but with little accuracy. McNeil had holstered the empty Colt and levered the Winchester. He aimed at Sommers, hoping to bring him down before the rancher made it inside the store. Instead, a bullet snapped the air past his head, and McNeil watched Sommers go to his hands and knees before reaching back and clutching the back of his bloody right thigh. McNeil glanced back over his shoulder and saw Sam leaning out the barn loft door brandishing his Winchester. Then McNeil glanced over his other shoulder, looking for Bud Long.

Long was calmly retreating toward the livery, firing his pistol held in his left hand. His right arm hung limply at his side, and his shirt sleeve was red with blood. Bullets splattered the mud at McNeil's feet. He turned and saw a cowboy with a rifle, standing on the far side of a tied horse, shooting at him from across the saddle. The cow pony crow hopped every time the rifle barked. McNeil squatted, took aim with the Winchester, and shot the cowboy's right leg exposed beneath the horse's belly. Then, when the man fell to the muddy ground on his side, McNeil shot him in the chest. The remaining ranch hands had recovered from their initial shock. They were finding the range, making it hot for McNeil, who was still in the middle of the street. So, he started backing toward the livery, returning fire as he went. A bullet struck McNeil in the upper right thigh as he reached the open door, but he didn't go down. Instead, hopping on his left leg, he hobbled on and passed through the doorway into the livery barn.

Bud long sat on an overturned bucket, reloading his Schofield with his left hand. He looked up at McNeil with a grimace. I got one in the arm, but it's only a scratch. McNeil hobbled over to him, favoring his right leg. He put the rifle down and ripped the sleeve off Long's shirt.

"Let me look."

"I'm fine. It's only a scratch."

"Looks like it went straight through the meat and missed the bone, but the bullet might have nicked an artery."

McNeil heard the whine of Sam's Winchester from the loft above and hoped the old man was keeping the remaining Bar Deuce hands at bay. He tore a strip off the tail of Long's shirt and folded it into a thick square. Then he pressed it to the exit wound on the backside of the marshal's right arm.

"Hold that for a second," he said.

Long pressed two fingers on the square of cloth. Then McNeil unknotted the bandana tied around Long's throat. He twisted it into a rope-like shape lengthwise and then bound it tightly around Long's upper arm, catching the makeshift bandage at the back of the wound. McNeil finished by knotting the rolled bandana on the front of Long's arm directly over the entry wound.

"That should hold it until Doc Holder can patch you up," McNeil said. "It has staunched the bleeding."

"Your leg is bleeding pretty bad too," Long said.

"I know it," McNeil said, unknotting his bandana and pulling it off his throat. Then he bound his thigh tightly with it.

"How many left?" Bud Long said. "I sort of lost track."

"Five maybe, counting Sommers," McNeil said after a quick mental calculation. "Sommers is shot twice, but I'm not sure how bad off he is. The last I saw of him, he broke into the mercantile up the street."

McNeil had just started reloading his Colt when he saw a shadow and looked up. Suddenly, a wild-eyed Charlie Watson had appeared framed in the open doorway. He pointed the pistol in his right hand at McNeil. Bud Long saw Watson a second after McNeil had and frantically struggled to bring his Schofield to bear, knowing he'd be a second too late. But Watson didn't pull the trigger. Instead, his body jerked, and he collapsed to the ground, revealing a wide-eyed Jay Lamar who had been standing behind Watson. In his right hand was a Remington Derringer, a small over-under, double-barrel .41 rim-fire hideout pistol, with smoke curling from the muzzle. Lamar looked down at Watson, whose luck had run out, and then his unsteady legs betrayed him, and he slumped to the ground, leaning against the door frame.

"I didn't know you had it in you, Jay," Long said matter-of-factly. "But I'm glad you happened by when you did."

McNeil shook his head and walked to the doorway to peek out. "It looks like the rest of those cowboys are still hunkering down up the street where they tied up their horses," he said. "That one must have worked his way down here from behind the buildings. I think I'll cross the street and do the same. I want to see if Sommers is still inside the mercantile. Sam is doing a good job keeping the heads of those cowpunchers down with his Winchester."

"I'll go with you," Long said, struggling to his feet.

"No, stay here, so you don't get that arm bleeding again. And watch Jay so that no one kills him. I've grown partial to him all of a sudden."

With that, McNeil hobbled across the street, impervious to the renewed gunfire coming from up the street. Then, making it safely across, he disappeared down the side of the hotel.

Chapter 28

Vengeance Served

As they neared Dead Horse Crossing, the men from the cattle herd could hear volleys of gunfire coming from the town. Wesley Cole pulled back on the reins to stop his horse and held up his hand, signaling the others to do the same.

"Miss Lamar, that's gunfire. Please wait here until we ride in and investigate," Cole said.

"I will do no such thing," Kate said, unlimbering her Henry rifle. "It's my town and my friends."

"Miss Lamar, I don't doubt your grit. But we have to ride hard. You'll lose your friend off that horse if you try to keep up. Also, I want my men to look after themselves, and you would be a distraction. So kindly stay behind until it's safe."

Kate looked back at Cotton's body strapped to the horse and then at Cole with indecision. "All right, Mr. Cole," she said finally. "But I'm following along slowly."

Cole nodded and turned to his men. "Let's ride."

The four cattlemen galloped away toward the town.

When McNeil hobbled along the side of the mercantile and peered around the front corner, one of Sommers' cowhands spotted him and started shooting. Bullets splintered the wood at the building's corner, forcing McNeil to back up. Then he drew the Colt, crept forward, and traded shots with the cowboy across the street. Suddenly, the shooting tapered off as quickly as it had started. Crouching, McNeil edged forward and peered around the corner again. Then he heard whooping and hollering. What he saw made his heart sink. Reinforcements had arrived. Four more cowboys were bearing down on the town at a gallop. Some of those firing from cover stood and looked gladly at the arriving galloping riders. They probably felt as relieved as McNeil felt dejected.

McNeil levered the Winchester, stepped out in the open, and drew a bead on the lead rider. As he took up the slack in the trigger, he stopped and removed his finger from it. McNeil recognized the man, Wesley Cole, one of his former trail bosses.

The riders all had their pistols in their hands, and as they drew close to the remnants of Sommers' crew, they opened fire and cut them down. The riders wheeled their horses in circles in the middle of the street until they had shot down the last survivor. From inside the mercantile, Sommers broke the glass out of a window and started firing a pistol at Cole and his men.

Fearing Sommers might shoot one of his newly arrived allies, McNeil leaned the rifle against the outside wall of the mercantile and, with his Colt in hand, threw his body against the store's front door, knocking it off his hinges. He landed on his right side on top of the busted door inside the store.

Sommers, his shirt and pants blood-soaked, sat next to the window with his back to the wall. Wide-eyed, he aimed his pistol at McNeil and fired. The bullet snatched McNeil's hat off his head. He snapped a quick shot at Sommers from his awkward position lying on his right side. The bullet found a peculiar target, taking off the thumb of Sommers' right hand at the joint before plowing into the wall beside him. Sommers dropped the pistol and then frantically scrambled to pick it up with his left hand. McNeil rolled into a sitting position, aimed his Colt at the center of Sommers' chest, and pulled the trigger. But the Colt clicked on a spent chamber. The gun was empty.

Wearing a hideous grin, Sommers aimed his pistol with his left hand and pulled the trigger. But it only clicked, also empty. Sommers feverishly reloaded with cartridges spilled on the floor beside him. McNeil did a border switch while getting to his feet. With the empty Colt in his left hand, he reached behind him and pulled the Walker Colt from the back of his gun belt. He thumbed back the hammer and shot Sommers in the chest. Cocking the heavy pistol again, he shot Sommers between the eyes. The rancher dropped his pistol. His head lolled to the side, and his forehead came to rest against the wall beside the window.

Wesley Cole jumped through the open doorway, gun drawn. He glanced at Sommers and then at McNeil.

"You all right, Murph?"

"Yeah, I'm okay, Wesley," McNeil said before going down to a knee, feeling the effects of the blood loss.

Two of Cole's drovers appeared in the ruined doorway. Turning to the men, Cole said, "Murph needs a doctor."

"I heard a doctor is working down at the livery," a drover said.

Cole nodded. "Pick Murphy up and get him down there, pronto."

The drovers, each with one of McNeil's arms across their shoulders, helped him back toward the livery. Cole and Phil Anderson followed, leading their horses. As they passed the body of Fitz Newsome, McNeil asked them to stop. He looked back at Cole.

"That man is wearing a badge that belongs to a friend. Could you get it for me, please?"

Nodding, Cole walked to the body and turned Newsome over with the tip of his muddy boot. Then, reaching down, he ripped the star off the dead man's shirt and handed it to McNeil. The men then continued to the livery stable.

As McNeil and the cattlemen arrived, Doc Holder had finished treating Bud's wound inside the barn. McNeil rubbed the badge on his shirt to clean the mud off.

"I've got something here that belongs to you, Marshal," he said, holding up the star.

Long's face broke into a wide smile, and McNeil pitched him the silver star. Catching it, Bud Long pinned it on his shirt.

"I guess I'm in the marshal business again," he said.

"You were never out of it, Bud," Doc Holder said with a smile.

"It takes more than a badge to make to a lawman, Marshal," McNeil said. "Far as I'm concerned, you never stopped being the marshal."

After examining McNeil's leg, Doc Holder announced the bullet was still in his thigh, and he'd have to remove it. But after declaring he was a medical doctor, not a veterinarian, he refused to operate inside a stable. Then, he directed the trail drivers to put McNeil on a horse and take him to his surgery.

Chapter 29

Aftermath

HAVING EXPERIENCED THE CHLOROFORM before, McNeil refused it when Doc Holder offered it this time. So with McNeil biting hard on a piece of thick leather, Holder probed the thigh wound with forceps and then extracted the bullet. Wesley Cole stood by, hat in hand, and waited patiently while the doctor cleaned and disinfected McNeil's wound. While Holder applied the dressing, he told McNeil a clean dressing would be required twice a day until the wound healed and that McNeil must stay off the leg for a while.

Afterward, Cole and McNeil talked, catching up on where they had been and what they had done since last seeing each other. Then Cole asked McNeil about his presence in Dead Horse Crossing and his name change. McNeil explained he had ridden to the town to check the welfare of a good friend, rancher Denton Everhart, at the request of his sister. McNeil then recounted how he learned about Sommers' intention to hoodwink a trail drive into buying his anthrax-infected cattle while determining what had happened to his friend.

"I didn't know your herd was the one coming," McNeil said. "Not that it would have mattered who it was. I still couldn't abide Sommers cheating honest men by selling them his sick cows."

"Well, I'm much obliged to you, Murph," Cole said.

"It was nothing any decent man wouldn't have done."

"How did you come by the name McNeil?"

"You've known me a long time, Wesley. When I set my cap to return to Texas, I naturally wanted to leave the past and reputation behind. So, I got into the habit of using other names to conceal my identity, and McNeil is only the latest moniker I've adopted."

Cole nodded knowingly. He knew all about the past and reputation of the man called Ian Murphy.

"So, what are you going to do now, Murph?"

"Not sure. A horse trader I've known for a spell, wired and offered to pay me to meet him in Denver and help him bring a string of mountain bred ponies back here to Texas. I was on my way there when I stopped here. But seeing as I'm so late now in keeping the appointment, I'm sure he's hired my replacement by now."

"Well, Murph, we've been over the river together and back numerous times. I've always got a job for a good cowpuncher. So why don't you sign on with us and help us push the herd up the trail to Denver? You can drive the hooligan wagon until your leg is well enough for you to sit a horse."

"Appreciate the offer, but I guess not, Wesley. I suppose I've swallowed enough trail dust and seen enough cow towns to last me a lifetime. I'm hoping to find a little quiet corner where I can buy some land and raise a few cows of my own."

"You intending to stay here in Dead Horse Crossing?"

"I guess not. There would be bad memories here on every corner. Not that I regret what I've done. Bull Sommers and his gunmen murdered my friend and another good man I met after getting here. Someone had to put an end to it."

"Well, I guess you did that and more. But you and a middle-aged town marshal against twelve guns? I must say, Murph, I admire your idea of fair odds."

McNeil grinned. "Well, if you and your boys hadn't shown up when you did, I'm not sure things would have turned out according to my plan."

"Glad we could help. Changing the subject, I haven't mentioned it to anyone here yet. But there is another herd three weeks behind mine, the last of the season. I reckon the anthrax break out will have burned itself out by the time they pass through here. Given the dire prospects this town faces, I'm inclined to wire Mr. Goodnight a recommendation to have his trail boss buy what cattle the ranchers here have left. Kate Lamar impressed me enough that I'd like to help her save her town."

"I'm sure she, along with the other folks hereabouts, would be in your debt, Wesley."

"All right, I'll have a word with Miss Lamar and send the wire on my way out of town."

After talking a while longer, Cole took his leave, eager to complete his business and rejoin his herd. The men shook hands.

"So long, Murph, or Mr. McNeil, I meant to say," Cole said with a twinkle in his eyes. "Maybe we'll meet again sometime up the trail somewhere."

"Maybe so, Wesley. I know it has been good to see you again this time. And, again, I'm mighty thankful for your help."

The men said goodbye, and Cole left Doc Holder's place, leaving McNeil alone with thoughts of his uncertain future.

A short while after Wesley Cole left, McNeil received another visitor, Kate Lamar. She entered Doc Holder's surgery with some trepidation, unsure how the man might receive her. But when he smiled, it lifted her heart considerably.

"Doc says you'll be your old ornery self before long."

"Yeah, the leg is sore, but I feel better already, in general."

"Good to hear," Kate said, pausing a beat.

"Well, I suppose you wondered where I went that day after I slipped out."

"Yes, I did at the time. But Wesley Cole filled me in. That took a lot of nerve to make that ride alone. And, I admit, it surprised me you carried the warning to them. When you disappeared, I was under the impression you were still partial to Sommers' plan."

"I was never partial to his plan. I only wanted this town to survive and was feeling pretty desperate. But after thinking about what you said that day, I knew you were right, and going along with Sommers was wrong."

"I guess I can understand why it was a hard decision for you, Kate. But in the end, you made the right choice."

"We found Cotton on the way back, and I brought him back for burial. We had the funeral this morning."

"I wish you had held off. I would have liked to attend. Cotton was a good man."

"Well, I have to say, he wasn't becoming any nosegay. Unfortunately, he died several days ago. We couldn't hold off on burying him. And, yes, he was a mighty good man. Probably better than you even know. When they ambushed him on the trail, Cotton stayed alive long enough to kill two of the coyotes who killed him."

"Can't say that surprises me. Patrick had sand. I would have liked knowing the man better."

Kate nodded. "Mr. Cole arranged for us to sell the surviving cattle to another herd coming through in a few weeks. He says the anthrax break out should be over by the time they arrive. I'm over the moon about that. So it looks like Dead Horse Crossing will survive another year at least."

"Yes, Wesley is a good man, and I'm glad he could help you and the town."

"You and Mr. Cole must be good friends. When I got there and told him of the circumstances when I left, I mentioned you. He recognized I was speaking of you right off, although he said he didn't know you by the name McNeil."

"Yes, Wesley Cole and I have been down the river many times. He knows me well."

"I don't suppose you want to tell me your true name."

"McNeil seems like a good name to me, and it's what I go by."

"Well, I suppose I hope you and I might get well enough acquainted that it would make sense for me to know who you truly are, Pete McNeil."

"Kate, I am the man that you know. And I'll be leaving Dead Horse Crossing for good in a few days, so it's unlikely we'll ever know one another better than we do now."

"Bud Long told me you mentioned wanting to get some land and raise cows," said wistfully. "You could do that right here in Dead Horse Crossing. I know of at least two spreads that have come available. And the people here wouldn't be sorry to see you stay."

McNeil shook his head sadly. "Like I told Wesley, I couldn't stay here. Every corner of this town would hold bad memories for me."

"I'll never understand your willingness to do what you did. But it needed to get done, and this town is lucky you did it. So, I don't see why you would hold bad feelings about it."

"Killing folks is nothing any decent man takes pride in doing," McNeil said. "And I take none in my actions here, though I agree someone had to do it. But memories of the trouble here in Dead Horse Crossing will always be bad ones for me."

"Including memories of me?"

"No, I'd say memories of you and a few of the others I've met will be the exceptions."

"Bud Long truly likes and respects you. So does Doc Holder."

"I feel the same about them."

"You know, Bud told me what my brother, Jay, did. It flabbergasted me. I wouldn't have believed that Jay could save himself, let alone someone else."

"People surprise you sometimes, Kate. Something like the trouble here comes along and acts as a crucible of sorts. It helps burn away the dross and refine a man until he emerges as the man he truly can be."

"Well, I'm sure glad he did what he did."

McNeil laughed a little. "That makes two of us. Getting shot once was one time too many."

"Where will you go now?"

"I'm not sure. But I feel partial to this country west of the Pecos. So, should you ever need me, Kate, I probably won't be so far away."

"I think I already do," Kate said, wiping away tears. "I wish I could change your mind about leaving."

"If anyone could, it would probably be you," McNeil said softly. "But I must go, and there is no changing it."

Kate sighed and nodded. Then she turned and left the room.

Chapter 30

A Cowboy Rides Away

WHEN MCNEIL WALKED DOWNSTAIRS from his room with his saddlebags over his shoulder, Bud Long and Doc Holder stood in the lobby waiting. McNeil walked to the desk and laid his room key on it.

"You can have your room back, Jay," he said with a grin.

Lamar nodded. "I'm sorry we were so rough on you when you arrived, Mr. McNeil. After all you did for this town, I'm powerfully sorry."

McNeil stuck out his hand, and Lamar took it. "No hard feelings on my part," he said. "I expect we all know each other better than we did then."

The men shook, and McNeil put the money on the desk to pay the rent.

Lamar pushed it back across the desk. "No charge," he said. "Least we can do."

"What will your boss say about it?"

"I am the boss," Jay said with a smile. "Bull Sommers bought this hotel shortly after he got here. So, I was working for him. But he died intestate, so I've taken over the place, and now I'm working for myself."

"Good for you. You're coming up the world, Jay. Just want to say thanks again for what you did."

"Mr. McNeil, you did far more for me. So it's me who should say thanks."

McNeil nodded. "Then we'll call her even. Take care of your sister, and good luck to you both."

"I'll be wishing you luck, too."

McNeil turned and crossed the room to Long and Holder.

"Thanks for patching me up, Doc."

"My pleasure. I suppose we can't change your mind about leaving? This town could use a solid citizen like you. There is no telling when we might have to battle a mess of desperadoes again."

"No, but I'm leaving you in good hands," McNeil said, winking at Long. "This town has a fine marshal, and I know he will keep things orderly." He extended his hand, and Holder shook it.

"Well, luck to you, son, wherever your travels take you."

"I appreciate it." McNeil turned to Bud Long, wearing a grin.

"Doc is right. You could stay, you know. The townsfolk wouldn't be sorry to have you stay."

McNeil smiled wryly. "They won't be sorry to see me go, either. The fight is over."

The marshal nodded. "Yes, your work is done here. But, I know everyone appreciates what you did for them."

"You did the hard work, Marshal. I only helped a little."

"Guess we'll agree to disagree on that one," Long chuckled.

The men shook hands.

"Vaya con Dios, cowboy."

"Adiós, Bud."

McNeil turned and walked out the door and descended the steps to the street. He threw his saddlebags over the back of his horse behind the saddle and tied them down.

"So long, Pete McNeil."

McNeil turned to see Kate Lamar standing on the boardwalk.

"Hello, Kate," he said, touching the brim of his hat. "Did you get that cattle deal squared away?"

"Yes, since Sommers had no relatives, the town is taking possession of what's left of the Bar Deuce herd. I've spoken to the other ranchers, and we expect we'll have close to the original fifteen hundred head to sell to that drive when they come through."

"You and Jay ought to consider taking over the spread."

"I'd like to, but the other ranchers have already carved up the Bar Deuce range. And they already have the stock to put on it."

"Well, how about the Lazy E?"

"To be honest, we can't afford to buy it from Denton's sister."

"If you're interested, I'd be glad to talk to Nancy on your behalf. She isn't the kind of woman who would want to move here and run a ranch. I suspect she might make a deal with you. Maybe you and Jay could pay her a little each year after selling your cattle."

"You think so?"

"Yes, I do. I'll have Nancy write to you in care of the hotel when I see her. Then you two can put your heads together and see what you can come up with."

"I'd be obliged, Pete. Maybe you could come back and see how we do?"

"Maybe so. If I ever make it out this way again, I just might."

McNeil turned, put a foot in the stirrup, and climbed aboard his horse. He tipped his hat. "Take care, Kate. Goodbye."

"Goodbye, Pete," she said sadly. Then she turned and hurried away.

McNeil rode to the edge of town and then stopped the horse at the gate of the old cemetery. He dismounted, tied up the horse, and walked through the gate. With all the new graves, it took a while, but he finally found Cotton Patrick's resting place. He took off his hat and held it in his hands.

"I didn't want to leave without saying goodbye and how sorry I am for the mistake I made that cost you your life. So, hopefully, you can hear me saying it. I have never decided about what I believe happens to us when we leave this world. But I hope you're out there somewhere listening and still have that smile it seemed you always wore. So long, pardner. Maybe I'll see you up the trail one day when my time comes."

McNeil turned away and put his hat back on. Then, at the gate, he climbed back into the saddle and headed south.

A lone rider on a long-legged roan left Dead Horse Crossing on the Pecos. He was a gray-eyed man wearing a black high-crowned, wide-brimmed hat, blue cotton shirt under a brown leather vest, and brown wool pants. He was riding easy when the people of the town watched him go.

About Author

RUSTY BEAUQUET is the pen name of a published American multi-genre writer of fiction, primarily known for his mystery & detective and police procedural novels. Beauquet, a retired Texas peace officer, grew up in Oklahoma and has lived much of his adult life in Texas. The Reckoning, the debut book in the new Lone Rider classic western series, is his first western novel. Rusty is an avid, lifelong fan of Louis L'Amour and Zane Grey and enjoys reading many of the other great writers of western fiction.